Coventry Tales

Our city, past and present, brought to life by some of Coventry's best-known authors and most exciting up-and-coming writers

Greenstream Publishing

Greenstream Publishing

Greenstream Publishing
12 Poplar Grove
Ryton on Dunsmore
Warwickshire
CV8 3QE
United Kingdom

www.greenstreampublishing.com
Published by Greenstream Publishing 2011

Paperback ISBN 978-1-907670-14-5
Kindle ISBN 978-1-907670-15-2
Copyright for this book edition is held by Coventry Writers' Group.
A catalogue record for this book is available from the British Library.

Table of Contents

Introduction

Michael Boxwell

Coventry. Is it a city in the shadows of Birmingham? Or à city of vision and purpose, with a proud history and a bright future? Earlier this year, I asked that question to a group of local writers – a group that includes some of Coventry's best-known storytellers. I asked them to come up with stories, poems and monologues inspired by our home city.

The response has been amazing. Local writers have been inspired to create stories and poems: insights from our past and our present; narratives that explore the fabric of our city and what makes it unique; stories that celebrate the character and life of Coventry and the people who inhabit her. Here you will find writing that will make you laugh and writing that will make you thoughtful. Above all, you will find stories and poems that remind all of us what makes Coventry special.

The very best entries are published here. Renowned local authors Ann Evans and Rosalie Warren are both represented, as is 'people's poet' Martin Brown, whose work will be well known to regular readers of the *Coventry Telegraph*.

Other writers may be less well known, yet their contributions are equally good. Time and time again, as I was reading through the entries, I was struck by how proficient our local writers are. Whether it is due to living in Coventry – perhaps the authorities have put something into the water? – or just pure coincidence, our local authors are arguably amongst the most talented in the land. So, once you've finished reading this book, why not seek out other books by our authors and enjoy those as well?

If you love Coventry and you enjoy storytelling and poetry at its very best, you will love this book. So sit back, relax and enjoy a good read.

Michael Boxwell
Commissioning Editor, *Coventry Tales*
November 2011

Living with Lady G:
A Husband's Story

As told to Margaret Egrot
Winning Entry in the 2011 Coventry Tales Competition

She was such a quiet little thing when I married her. Still in her teens. Lovely golden hair. A sweet face. I quite took to her from the start – glad her brother came up with the idea, even if at the time he only wanted the marriage to go through so I'd support his bid to be Sheriff of Lincoln and he could get his widowed little sister off his hands. I don't get on with him too well myself. He has old-fashioned views about women – thinks they are weak willed and only too ready to flaunt themselves unless they have a man to keep them in check, whereas I'm a bit more progressive in my outlook. Still, as brothers-in-law go, he's not too bad really – and the dowry was good.

Godiva – lovely name, means 'Gift of God', you know. And she really was like a gift of God to me. Certainly, the money she brought with her helped me sort the plumbing out in the manor. She was obliging in the bedroom, too, and we soon got our heir and spare sorted. She's not so keen now – more into good causes – but she turns a blind eye when she needs to (know what I mean?), so I don't do too badly.

But it's all these good causes that have been causing me grief recently. Not only has she been giving her own money away – she wants me to give mine away, too. She thinks it's part of being an earl in this modern age. So here we are, both benefactors of this new monastery in Coventry. Which is OK by me – after all, it's where we live and it looks good in the eyes of God and all that, and I'm all for laying down the foundations in

3

this life for a comfortable berth in the next one. And it gives me a bit of a buzz in the here and now, too, to be honest, when I see my coat of arms, and dedications to me, everywhere you look round Coventry. Even if it is only a piddling little place; not at all like London. But it's growing – and a big thanks to my sheep and cloth manufacture for that, too. Oh yes, the people of Coventry have a lot to thank me for.

Anyway, things started to get out of hand on the wife front. Not content with making us benefactors in Coventry – where people can see us and be properly appreciative, she was donating her – our – my – money all over the shop: here a monastery in Worcester, there a minster in Lincoln, another in Leominster, then one in Chester – the list just goes on and on. And she's been parting with her jewellery, too – not that I mind some going to the cathedral in Coventry, for obvious reasons, and it's just good business sense to get some into St Paul's in London if we want to drum up more markets for our wool down there. But why Evesham for God's sake? And last year I found out that she and her sister, Wulviva (horrible name), have gone and given a manor to the cathedral in Hereford – where they've got their own wool producers directly in competition with us who should be divvying up.

It's difficult to say anything to her. As I said – I did say, didn't I? – she's a good wife really. Still looks good in a gown, all her own teeth, lovely long hair – I know she dyes it these days (she thinks I don't know so I'm not letting on) but when she lets it down of an evening to brush it out before she retires to her own bedroom – well, it falls right down to her waist. Still gives me a bit of a stirring, that – her in nothing but a shift, her hairbrush moving so rhythmically up and down her long golden tresses, and that slow sweet smile she has when she finally stops her good deeds for the day and relaxes.

4

Maybe I should have spoken to her at one of these times, when she was sitting still for a moment. Pointed out to her that the money was running out – we couldn't keep giving out to the church without getting money in, and there's no money in sheep these days – too many jumped-up yeomen from the West Country getting in on the act and bringing prices down. But I kept quiet and looked to other ways to fund her charity.

Like taxes. Those get a good return for the effort. I just decide what I can put a levy on and then employ a few chaps to go round collecting the money. First up were horses (though I had to add donkeys quickly, as people soon tried a bit of tax avoidance by swapping their pack horses for asses). That earned us quite a bit, but after her last donation – to an abbey in Much Wenlock, of all places – we were almost down to our last bag of groats.

So I hit on the idea of taxing every household in Coventry – a sort of extra ground rent, so to speak. After all, everybody has got to have somewhere to live, even if it's only a hovel, and they are all on my land. OK, they didn't like it, but to me it was that or tell the wife she couldn't make any more donations. And to tell the truth, I'm more scared of her than them.

It worked well for a while, too. But the trouble with Lady G is, she likes to be loved by the people as well as keeping in with God and watching out for our eternal souls. She takes food parcels to the sick and needy, and she found there were more and more sick and needy on her list as the year went on. So she started to ask questions. And they told her it was all because of her husband's new taxes.

Then she started on me. Wouldn't listen to reason. I couldn't get her to get her head round the fact that it was these self-same taxes that provided her with the money for the food parcels. Wouldn't contemplate giving up her charitable

5

donations and endowments so that we could live like earls within our means.

She just went on and on at me. Day after day, week after week. "Leofric, I will not honour your bed until you lift the taxes on the poor people of Coventry," she said once. (That's a laugh – it's been a good few years now since we've had any of that, but I digress.) After a month of daily nagging – God, that woman can be stubborn at times – I was truly exasperated.

"Okay, okay!" I said, "You win."

She gave me a huge smile and I swear she was about to kiss me.

But I held up my hand. "You win," I repeated, "on one condition. If you care that much about your precious downtrodden masses, you must prove it to me by riding stark naked through the town centre in broad daylight."

Well, that put the ball back into her court. I didn't get the kiss and she left the room quickly. Great, I thought, she'll never compromise her modesty and I will get a bit of peace at last. Bliss!

First day of the month, I sent the tax collectors out as usual. And they came back with the usual money. Not a lot – they live meanly, those Coventry town people so I can't expect to be a rich man on their dues. But it's enough to keep the manor running – and the wife in donation money. But my chief collector gave me a nasty shock.

"This is your last collection," he said.

"What?" I exploded. "What do you think I'm paying you for?"

He looked a bit shifty then, shuffling from foot to foot.

"Well, spit it out, man," I prompted him.

"It's Her Ladyship, Your Lordship," he said eventually. "She says she's done a deal with you and she is to ride naked through the streets of Coventry, and then you won't charge any more taxes."

I sat down heavily. The little minx! My brother-in-law was right after all. But I never thought my own dear wife was like that.

What to do? I summoned her straight away to forbid her to proceed with this folly, but she replied she was merely carrying out my condition for abolishing what she kept calling my excessive taxation.

She had it all arranged. She had instructed all the tax collectors (my tax collectors!) to tell everyone to keep indoors with the shutters down next Wednesday morning, as she would be riding her favourite white horse from one end of the market to the other, wearing nothing but her long fair hair, so as to hold me to a promise to lift the tax burden on them.

There was nothing I could say to stop her. I was hoist by my own petard, so to speak. Wednesday came and I decided to make myself scarce. I went fishing with a few close retainers (and tried to ignore their obvious reluctance to miss seeing her ladyship set off – great grief, she's old enough to be their mother for some of them).

I came back late that evening. I'd caught nothing but a cold, and I was a bit the worse for wear, too, to be honest. Lady G was still up, and clad in her best evening gown. She gave me her usual gentle smile, but did I note a glint of triumph in her eye?

"Well?" I asked her.

"It's done," she replied.

"How will I know?" I asked cunningly, "Seeing as everyone was indoors and told not to look."

"One did," she replied. "The tailor, Tom something or other. You can ask him."

"The dirty old man!" I expostulated. "How dare he look at my wife like that? He must be punished."

"He already has been," she said. "As soon as I passed where he was peeping, he was struck blind. He won't be able to work anymore now."

I was a little mollified to hear this, but I still harrumphed a bit and rubbed my head.

"Perhaps you'll feel better after supper," said Lady G. "I've ordered your favourite."

So there it was. My wife had fulfilled what I had thought was an impossible condition; now I had to keep my part of the bargain. No more taxes – and the manor roof repairs would have to wait for a good few more years. She'll just have to keep putting the pans out in the great hall every time it rains.

Bit by bit, Lady G and I have settled back into a companionable way of life. She's cut down a little on her donating, and I have to spend a bit more time worrying over the accounts, but we're happy enough. And the townsfolk? God, they were ecstatic after that ride – still are. Seem to regard Lady G as a saint or something. They'll be carving a bloody statue of her next – and then quarrelling about where to put it for centuries to come.

Gallows Day

Margaret Mather
Second Place in the 2011 Coventry Tales Competition

"Mary Ball, you have been found guilty of wilful murder. You poisoned your husband, Thomas Ball, by administering arsenic to him. You will be taken to a place of execution where you will be hanged by the neck until you are dead. This will take place tomorrow, the Ninth Day of August Eighteen Forty-Nine at ten o'clock in Pepper Lane, Coventry.

"Do you have anything to say?"

"No sir," Mary whispered.

"Take the prisoner down."

The judge stood up, took the black cloth from his head and placed it on the table. Without a backward glance he left the room.

Mary was half-dragged, sobbing, to the cells. Two burly prison guards opened the room and unceremoniously threw her in. She heard the ominous grating of a key turn in a rusty lock and the gleeful voices of the prison guards as they stumbled up the dimly lit corridor.

"It should be a right good hanging; twenty thousand people I've heard tell are coming to see her drop."

"Many are coming from her home town, Nuneaton. People from Bedworth have already started walking. There's nothing they like better than a good hanging."

"They say it's to be the last ever female public hanging in Coventry."

"Aye, John, everyone will want to be part of that."

"I'm taking the wife and kids. What about you, Will?"

9

"Wouldn't miss it for the world. Food's already packed."
Their voices drifted away until all that could be heard
were faint mumblings.

The room smelt of rotting cabbage; it was filthy and the stub of a
candle stood in the middle of a wooden table. Straw covered the
stone floor. Mary didn't take much notice of her surroundings.
Her head felt as if it would burst as she tried to take in the
enormity of the position she found herself in.

How had it come to this? At the age of 31, here she was in
prison, condemned to die for a crime she did not commit. Who
would look after her daughter? What was to become of her? She
was only four years old. The only thing left for her now would
be the workhouse, and Mary cursed the day that she had caught
the eye of her child's father.

She lay down on the cold stone floor and tried to get
some sleep.

She must have drifted off, and woke with a start to find a
man dressed in black shaking her roughly by the shoulders.

"Wake up, you stupid girl, wake up," he shouted in her
ear.

Mary rubbed the sleep from her eyes and, as she became
more aware, noticed that the candle was alight and two chairs
were placed at the table. The candle threw long shadows into the
corners of the small cell. A shiver ran through her and she began
to shake uncontrollably.

"Mary Ball, I am the prison chaplain and I've come to ask
you to put your mark on this confession."

Mary was startled. "Why do you want a signed
confession? I have already been found guilty."

"You have professed your innocence all through your
trial. I need a proper confession, one that will show how right

we were to hang you. Now, make your mark upon this paper, girl, and be quick about it." The chaplain handed her a quill.

"I can't do that, sir, as I did not poison my husband."

"Well now, that's a great pity because I need a confession and I can guarantee that before the sun rises, I shall have it."

Mary wasn't sure how he would do that, but she had heard some gruesome stories about the torture that went on in these places. The tone of his voice terrified her and she knew that whatever he had in mind would not be pleasant.

"Come over here, girl; sit on that chair."

Mary did as ordered.

He sat opposite her. His dark eyes seemed to probe into her soul. She could smell ale on his breath and gave an involuntary shiver.

"Now give me your hand."

She did as asked. His grip was as hard as iron. Reaching for the candle, he pulled it close and at the same time lifted her hand into the air. Mary could tell by the speed of his hand that he had done this many times before. The candle was placed directly under her arm. She could feel the heat and tried to pull away, but he tightened his grip. Her flesh started to bubble and a smell akin to burnt pork reached her nostrils as a searing pain ran through her body.

She screamed. He carried on burning her flesh over the naked flame, oblivious to her cries of pain.

"Please let go of my arm, I beg of you, sir," she pleaded.

He grinned at her and said, "Confess and I'll stop. You have nothing left to lose."

She knew he was right.

"Please stop, and after you have listened to my sorry tale, I will make my mark."

"Carry on. I have all night," he sneered, releasing the grip on her arm.

11

Mary quickly pulled her arm back. Blisters had started to form and they were very painful. She was not going to let it show and in a quiet, dignified voice, she began to tell him about the events that led up to this horrific moment.

"I was the daughter of Isaac Wright and Alice Ward. My father was the innkeeper of the White Hart Inn, Market Square, Nuneaton. My mother died in childbirth.

"Blaming me for my mother's death, my father made sure that I would cook, clean and wait on tables from an early age. I had to endure the sly touches from his customers when he wasn't looking, the beatings for lying when I told him what they had done and the awful loneliness. He never married again but plenty of women shared his bed.

"He would make me sleep in the kitchen with the dogs and woe betides if I ventured upstairs for any other reason than to clean. I wanted to escape this life, and when Thomas Ball told my father that he would take me off his hands for a small fee, he agreed, and I thought anything would be better than this life of drudgery.

"I was wrong. Thomas Ball took great delight in using me as a punch bag. Even when I was nine months pregnant he would take his belt to me in one of his drunken rages. I lost five babies due to his beatings. I began to think that I would never have any children. Then, when I was eight months pregnant with my last child, my father took seriously ill. He insisted that I move back in for a month or so to look after him and he bribed Thomas with a free glass or two of ale every night. That gave me just enough time for my daughter to be born without the constant threat of beatings.

"She was a beautiful baby, but it wasn't long before the beatings started again, and when he had punched me senseless he would turn his attentions to our daughter. I tried my best to protect her. At the start of one of my husband's rages I would send Mary Ann outside to play in the street. It was safer there than in her own home."

Mary looked up into the face of the prison chaplain and thought that she saw pity there, as if he realised that she was someone who had been greatly mistreated by everyone she had ever come into contact with. He looked ashamed now of his torture, but Mary guessed he would soon be justifying himself by thinking that if he hadn't done it, someone else would have.

"I hated my husband, loathed him with every breath that I took. I wished him dead many, many times but kill him, no, I didn't kill him – he killed himself.

"Yes, I bought the arsenic from the chemist in Market Square and yes, I sat the bottle on the mantelshelf, but it was to kill bugs. I always put it high up, out of reach from my daughter. Thomas came home late; he was drunk and smelt of perfume from his latest woman. I had never seen him so drunk. He fell asleep on the chair and I went to bed happy in the knowledge that at least for one night my daughter and I would be safe.

"When I awoke the next morning I found Thomas lying on the floor clutching a blue glass bottle. In his drunken stupor, he had picked it up, believing it to be stomach salts. I took the bottle from his hand and hid it in my apron before sending for the doctor, because I knew that I'd get the blame.

"Everything would have been fine, if someone hadn't decided to tell the police that I had been heard in the street shouting at him, "I'll do for you!" They decided on a post-mortem and, analysing his stomach contents, found more than the usual amount of arsenic.

"All my life I have fought so desperately hard, but when I heard the knock on the door and opened it to find the police standing there, I knew right there and then that my life was over. I would never see my daughter again.

"The only thing I can do for her now is to go to my death with grace and dignity."

The tears poured down her cheeks as she lifted her eyes to look into the face of her tormentor.

"I believe you, Mary, but I cannot do anything about it. I can, however, promise you that I will find a kindly family to look after your daughter and that she will be well cared for."

"Thank you sir, that's all I can hope for."

Mary made her mark on the paper.

The day of the execution was sunny with a slight breeze; ideal hanging weather.

The roads from Nuneaton and Bedworth where full of men, women and children, some riding, some walking. Laughter and music filled the air and a real gala day atmosphere was everywhere. There were peddlers on every street corner selling their wares; the smell of hog roast and fresh bread filled the nostrils as you passed. People were placing bets on how long it would take Mary to die. The Golden Cross Inn had never been so busy. They couldn't fill the jugs of beer quickly enough.

Mary had walked the floor of her cell all night and, although exhausted, she knew it wouldn't be long before she could leave this cruel world behind. In a resigned fashion, she longed for ten o'clock to come, the time when the noose would be placed around her neck and all of her past pain would disappear.

She could hear the laughter and the music from the crowd outside and hoped that she didn't disappoint. Her only regret – Mary Ann, her daughter.

The prison chaplain entered Mary's cell along with two guards. He found it difficult to look at her after listening to her story last night.

The guards shackled her arms and legs with heavy chains.

14

"Please sir, what will happen to my body after I'm dead? Will there be a grave and a headstone for my daughter to visit?"

The chaplain looked at Mary and with almost a hint of pity in his voice he said, "I'm sorry but your body will be buried upright in an unmarked grave, underneath the cobbles, beyond the grounds of Holy Trinity Church. All murderers must be buried upright so that they may never rest in peace. A death mask will be cast of your face and will be placed on a pole for everyone to look at in quiet contemplation. There will be no headstone."

It was a short walk from the gaol to the gallows in Pepper Lane.

Mary summoned from deep within all of the strength and dignity needed to see her through the next ten minutes. As she stepped up to the gallows, there was a hush from the huge crowd. They held their breath, the rope was placed over her head and the trapdoor opened. Mary's body jerked once or twice like a puppet on strings and then stopped.

The crowd erupted.

Upon A Time

Mary Ogilvie

Winding entries
dirty newspapers
scattered all around,
now you see
now you don't see
your childhood all around,
before you dash away
and grow up
little do you know
of the peace that you
have left behind
in the warmth of that
old road.

Wonders of the Coventry Ring

Rosalie Warren

Third Place in the 2011 Coventry Tales Competition

Dedicated to three of my heroes: Professor Brian Cox, Sir
Patrick Moore and the late and very great Douglas Adams

*Professor Brian Bramley, physicist and superstar, presents a TV
documentary on a phenomenon that has baffled generations of
scientists – the Coventry Ring.*

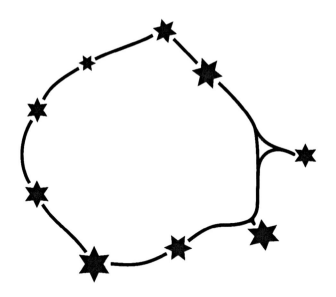

Exterior: Coventry, sunset.
*We see the silhouette of a helicopter against the reflective
golden surface of Coventry's AXA building, as the setting sun
dissolves in a blood-red splurge against the low-lying clouds.
Professor Brian Bramley, youthful cosmologist of the airwaves,*

17

stands dangerously close to Junction 9 in his Arctic jacket (this is April, after all), gazing into camera with wonder in his eyes as the sky darkens behind him and then takes on a fuzzy orange glow.

Professor Brian Bramley:
Welcome to *Wonders of the Coventry Ring*, the last in my current series of documentaries, where I will once again try to impress you with the hushedness of my voice, the flutteriness of my eyelashes, the slimness of my hips and, er... what was the other thing?

   [*Under his breath*] *Shoot, I forgot my bucket and spade. Do I need my bucket and spade for this bit, Martin?*

   No? OK, then. The Coventry Ring – one of the unexplained mysteries of the universe, about to be revealed to you...

   [*Under his breath, once more*] *Where's the music? What happened to my backing track? What? He didn't? Sir Patrick Thaw, of all people? Master of the xylophone himself, and he won't let me play my keyboards? Things can only get worse, that's all I can say. What? Oh, that comes later, when we get onto the Ring Road? OK, Marts... cut all that...*

Tonight, we leave the graininess of gravity, the exertions of the elements and the luciferousness of light to turn to that most intriguing of all unanswered questions – what, why, who, how and where is the Coventry Ring?

   This question has mystified the scientific community ever since the unearthly phenomenon first appeared on the Coventry skyline in the late 1960s, not long after the infamous Big Bung, which created the black hole that lies at the very centre of the UK, only twenty miles from Coventry and colloquially known as Brum.

Sir Patrick Thaw, he of the xylophone and the inability to appreciate any music composed since 1962, first spotted traces of the Coventry Ring with his homemade spoon-refracting Gellerscope, in his garden in Sussex, one stormy night in 1971. Sophisticated triangulation techniques showed its position to be dead in the (dead) centre of Coventry city. No, that's unfair – Coventry still had signs of life at that time. Or at least, Coventry City did...

Anyway, Sir Patrick conducted detailed investigations and concluded that the Coventry Ring was an extra-terrestrially induced construction that could not possibly have been created by the human mind (or, indeed, by the mind of God, assuming that God is good, which I don't have time to go into here).

Either it was a natural event on a par with the Big Bung itself or – hang on, I need my bucket for this one – [*eyelash flutter, last rays of sun just catching BB's blue plastic bucket*] – or it was the work of visitors from... outer space!

I know. I'm impressed, too. By my eyelashes, I mean, and my slinky hips. To say nothing of my bucket. If you could only hear the backing track...

Anyway, back to the Ring. No, no, Marts – not the Wagner. The Coventry Ring, I mean – and yes, ladies, since you ask, I'm married [*flashes wedding ring to camera*]. Sorry an' all that...

To cut a long story short, we believe that the Coventry Ring is a particle accelerator built by aliens from Zug-Blatter-6 [*thanks, Douglas, me old mate*] in order to fire opposing beams of particles called Jag-Uar bosons at each other so that they effectively collide at nearly twice the speed of light. The Jag-Uar boson was originally manufactured in the Zug-Blatterians' factory near Coventry airport and was named after its Zuggian creators, Professor Mick Jag and his student, Heah Uar.

The burst of energy produced when a beam of Jag-Uars hits a beam of anti Jag-Uars (same mass, same charge, but cost three times as much) was enough to create a sonic boom known ever after as the Ska Boom and immortalised in the music of The Specials [*sudden burst of Ska*]. Haha, Sir Patrick, you didn't see that one coming. Play that on your xylophone if you can!

It was also known as the ka-boom or car-boom, which reverberated through Coventry until the nineteen-eighties, when the Jag-Uar bosons started to lose their momentum (and their position), owing to interference from a major galactic disaster known as the Thatcher Overdrive. But that's another programme...

Anyway, we have two opposing beams of Jag-Uar bosons – we have a boom – a boomtown, we have rats, we have.... [*burst of 'Tell me why...'*] – oh heck, Patrick, you were too quick for me thurr. Anyway, I love Mondays – it's the day I get to look through me mate Martin's telescope.

In experiments like this, there's always a certain degree of contamination by smaller particles; the boring ones that move much more slowly. Escort particles, we call them – struggling to keep up. Fiestas, Micras and Minis. And Polos – they're the ones with the hole in the nucleus due to radioactive decay. And, of course, there's always the Whyte-Vann lepton, chiefly distinguished by its negative values of charm, politeness and common courtesy. And its unpredictable speed, direction, position and momentum, and its tendency to follow much too close behind other particles. This is known as Tayle-Guyting, after pioneering Whyte-Van researchers Wilbur Tayle and Joshua Guy Ting.

Strange effects have been observed when a Whyte-Vann lepton encounters one of the smaller and less confident particles such as the Micra. Micra particles have been known to dissolve away in sheer terror when being Tayle-Guyted by a Whyte-Vann

lepton, an unlawful act which necessitates regular patrols of the
Coventry Ring by the particle police, a jovial band of plodders
who try to enforce the so-called velocity limit of the Ring – the
value of which, unfortunately, remains unknown.

The Ring is one of
those wild and woolly areas
of the universe called LUTs
– or 'laws unto themselves'.
It gives rise to strange
effects not observed
elsewhere. For example,
one bewildering feature of
the Ring is that it circles the
city of Coventry on the
inside. Honest, it does. It's
as though the earth were suddenly to dive into the sun and
continue its merry orbit in among the hydrogen and helium
nuclei, oblivious to the hectic fusion going on all around (very
like Far Gosford Street, I'm told, on a Saturday night). Or as if
an electron were suddenly to burrow into the nucleus of an atom
rather than keep to the outside. Breaks all the laws of physics,
yet you've only to stand here by bl**dy freezing Junction 9 to
see it all happen.

I'm told that if the flow of particles around the Ring were
ever to stop, then life as we know it in Coventry would come to
an end. (I'd happily press the switch but no one will tell me
where it is...) If worryingly low radiation levels are detected on
the Ring, particles called taxions are released at Junction 6, just
by the railway station. Taxions are similar to Whyte-Vann
leptons in their negative values for charm and politeness, with
the added irritation that their speed is very slow. So slow, in fact,
that the laws of relativity break down, the internal constituents
of the taxions lose mass (in a process known as vomiting) and

time speeds up to a ridiculous degree. Taxion time is measured by a device known as a 'fare meter', which expresses distance in pounds sterling, the smallest quantifiable unit of which is the five-pound note.

The Second Law of Taxidurrnamics tells us that taxions travel slowest (and hence time travels fastest) at night – which means that after 10pm the quantum unit of distance is the tenner.

And while we're at it, the Third Law of Taxidurrnamics says that action and reaction are equal and opposite – i.e., if Coventry City scores, the opposing team will always score within the next minute. Sadly, the effect is not reversible and, if the other team scores first, the chances are that Coventry will not score back, ever. This is known as Ricoh symmetry-breaking, and if you're a City supporter it's a bl**dy shame.

The First Law? Well, since you ask, it's all about Schrödinger's cat, which unfortunately wandered into the Ring in 1983, promptly died, and was rediscovered stuffed inside a glass case in the Herbert Museum in 1997. We are talking taxidurrmy, after all.

Then there's Heisenberg's Indecisiveness Principle – which says that he (or perhaps she) who hesitates on the Ring is lost.

There are the not-so-small black holes, called pot-holions, which have been known to swallow a Micra particle whole and regurgitate it in another dimension in the form of a Sko-Da boson.

And there's that ghostly quantum phenomenon to end them all – entrance/exit duality (or "Is this slip road the entrance or the exit, mate? What, both at once? Aaaahhhggrrrhhh!") Without getting too religious, this is, to my mind, the biggest piece of evidence against the existence of God. Who, let's face it, if He'd wanted us to play dice, would have given us furry cubic hands with numbers on the faces. It goes against intelligent design, too. Intelligence and the Coventry Ring are mutually exclusive – just ask Heisenberg.

Entrance/exit duality is related to the more familiar 'wave/particle duality' – where a wave may be construed to be (a) a particle or (b) a signal that you are being let into the stream of traffic, whereas in fact the driver was making a rude gesture at you.

And finally – there's Inflation. This is the period of rapid expansion of the city that occurred shortly after the construction of the Coventry Ring. It explains (a) the remarkably uniform distribution of fast-food outlets in Coventry city centre and (b) the extortionate cost of petrol and fast food. To say nothing of taxions and cats...

[Final flutter of BB's eyelashes and waving of bucket and spade]

Well, that just about wraps things up. I hope I've convinced you that the Coventry Ring is one of the wonders – if not *the* wonder – of the universe. I've failed to find any sand around here for building castles, but I'm off now to annoy some swans in the Coventry canal.

After which, I'll probably sit down and stare at an ancient Jag-Uar boson, as it very slowly rusts away in one of the abandoned factories of Coventry.

[Strains of keyboards being played. A voice sings 'Things can only get worse...' or something very similar. And, faintly at first but slowly gaining volume, the tinkling of a xylophone joins in.]

This Town

Martin Brown

Much travelled have I been
Around this town of ours;
From Foleshill's rugged mountain peaks
To Finham's cloud-capped towers.

The Pyramids of Wyken,
The Caves of Eastern Green,
The Hanging Gardens of Tile Hill;
All these things I've seen.

The Redwood trees of Radford
Where kites and eagles nest,
The waterfalls of Willenhall,
These rank amongst the best.

Binley's wild savannah,
Across which zebras trot,
The Aztec ruins of Whoberley,
Yes, I've seen the lot.

But I keep these things a secret,
And so, I think, should you.
Or we'll be swamped by tourists,
Who'll want to see them too.

Inspired

Ann Evans

Have you ever wondered how the ancient, tall spire of Coventry's old cathedral escaped Hitler's bombs in the Second World War?

Thousands of bombs fell on the city centre and most of the city's beautiful buildings were destroyed or damaged. The cathedral itself, once known as Saint Michael's Church, was utterly devastated.

But the spire remained. Intact. Safe!

Have you ever wondered what kept it safe?

I know, you see. I know its secret, and it is a huge secret. But you look trustworthy. Perhaps I can tell you, if I whisper it softly. Come closer and I will tell you a strange but true tale. One that goes back more than a thousand years.

Oh, I can see that look of disbelief on your face. You're wondering how I – a mere girl of fourteen – can hold such a secret. Well, let me tell you that I can, because the story – this one-thousand-year-old story – involves me. I am at its very heart.

My name is Megan – at least that is my 21st century name. But in my past life, when I lived in the 13th century, my name was Celeste.

I was born in the year 1208 AD, the daughter of a stonemason. I had a younger sister named Ruth. We lived just a few miles from the centre of Coventry, or Coueantree, as it was known then.

In our village was a woman named Talitha. She looked younger than my mother; she never seemed to age. There was a rumour that the pendant she wore around her neck was magical and kept her young. But I didn't believe that... not at first, anyway.

One day Talitha was weeping – grieving for an old woman in our village who had died of old age. Poor Talitha's heart seemed to be breaking.

No one understood why she was grieving so badly – until, in the middle of the night, Talitha crept into our house, tiptoed in while my family were sleeping. She put her finger to her lips, begging me to stay silent.

I was curious. She knelt beside my bed and explained that the pendant she wore was indeed magical. It possessed the power of immortality. She told me that 184 years ago, she had been the handmaid to Godiva, and this pendant, known as the Cross of Aes Dana, had been given to her for safekeeping.

It seemed that Godiva had, for many years, kept it safe by placing it over the statue of Saint Osberga in St Mary's Church. But now, as she was growing old, she feared it would fall into evil hands when she died.

Godiva explained to Talitha that the Cross of Aes Dana had been created by pagans, whose powerful sorcerers enchanted it with the gift of everlasting life. It had been guarded over the centuries by just a handful of people who aged swiftly once it was removed from them (by fair means or foul!)

That night, as I listened to Talitha, she explained how Godiva had begged her to keep it safe. Talitha had not let Godiva down. She kept the pendant safe – she wore it around her own neck for almost 200 years.

Earlier that day, when we had puzzled why Talitha was weeping so bitterly over the death of an old woman, we hadn't known the old woman was Talitha's great great great granddaughter.

As Talitha knelt by my bed that night, she whispered to me, "Celeste, do you know how many children, grandchildren and great grandchildren I have seen born, grow up and die? Can you imagine the heartache I have suffered?"

I could imagine. And it made me want to weep.

Then Talitha took the pendant from her neck and said, "I have done my duty to Godiva. I can bear this burden no more. Please take it, Celeste, and hide it. Hide it away from the clutches of Friar Lucius and people like him. Friar Lucius is evil and for a long time he has been after this cross. But please, dear Celeste, do not wear it. I would not wish that burden on you."

Leaving me with the Cross of Aes Dana, Talitha then rose from her knees. I saw that her movements were slow now, as if her joints ached. And her soft, smooth skin was beginning to gather lines and wrinkles. The years – the 184 years that she had worn that magical cross – were swiftly catching up on her. And as she shuffled from my house that night, I realised that it was a very, very old lady leaving.

By morning, Talitha was dead.

Not only dead but rotted away to just a skeleton.

Our village was in shock. They carried her body from the house reverently in a box, but they could just as easily have put her remains in a sack and slung it over someone's shoulder – so little was left of poor Talitha.

My sister Ruth and I picked meadow flowers for her grave – 184 flowers, one for every year of her life. But as Ruth was away fetching a pot to put the flowers in, I felt a shadow fall over me. I looked up to see Friar Lucius almost upon me.

My heart jumped into my throat. Here was the evil Friar Lucius, who was desperate to get his clutches on the Cross of Aes Dana, and there was I, keeper of the cross for just a few hours and already fearing that he would know, and steal it from me.

As Friar Lucius towered over me, I sensed the evil in him. His face was white, his robes were black as his heart and he clasped his hands together as if in prayer, as if he were a holy man, a man of God. But I knew he should not be wearing the robes of the church. He was pure evil – and I was afraid.

"Child," he said to me, his face so close I could smell his foul breath. "I hear the dead woman wore a pendant but when they buried her there was no sign of it. Do you know where it is?"

"No!" I answered, feeling my face scorching as I lied.

He knew I was lying and leaned closer. "Do you know it's a sin to lie, child?" he warned. "And sinners burn in hell. Do you want to burn in hell, child?"

My heart was thudding and I wanted to run, but I knew I had to stay calm and pretend to know nothing. Defiantly, I said, "Probably her pendant rotted away, like the rest of her."

His cold eyes warned me that he knew I was lying and as soon as I could, I ran from him, desperate to find somewhere to hide the Cross of Aes Dana.

In the distance I saw the tall spire of Saint Michael's Church.

I bided my time, and when no one was watching I took my father's hammer and chisel. I had watched him working with stone. I knew how to wield these tools.

I was exhausted after climbing the 300 steps to the balcony of the spire. But oh! The views over the countryside took my breath away. The rivers were like silver ribbons and the fields like a giant patchwork blanket spread over the earth to keep it warm.

I had no time to waste. I chose a brick and chiselled it from an inner wall. Making a small cavity, I tucked the pendant

28

away and slid the brick back into place. I held it fast with the chippings. Then, blowing the red dust to the wind, I ran back down the stone steps and out into the fading evening sunset.

And straight into the evil clutches of Friar Lucius.

My memories of my life as Celeste, the daughter of a stonemason back in the 13th century, stop from that moment on. And when I, Megan, moved here to Coventry with my parents less than a year ago, when Dad got a new job here, I had no memories of this previous existence at all.

Only gradually, I started having feelings of *déjà vu*. Memories of faces, people and words ran through my head, confusing and frightening me.

When I started my new school, I couldn't understand why I thought I knew a particular girl in class...

Until I realised she was my little sister, Ruth. But that was insane. I don't have a little sister!

For a while, I really thought I was going crazy. And then things started to get worse.

I started to feel like I was being haunted by the ghost of a monk. This dark sinister presence kept whispering in my ear – asking me where I had hidden it.

Hidden what? I wanted to scream.

By now, my parents were starting to think I'd gone insane.

But then I started to remember. Bit by bit. Memories unfolding like I was turning back the pages of an ancient book.

I finally remembered what I had hidden and where I had hidden it.

My memories from when I was Celeste end abruptly when Friar Lucius leapt out from the trees as I was running home that evening. But he didn't get the Cross of Aes Danas from me. He couldn't have, because the spire where I hid it is still standing.

I know why the cathedral spire is still standing, despite the ravages of time, storms and bombings.

And now... so do you.

Coventry Unquiet:
A Tale of Urban Haunting

Chris Jarvis

People ask me how I got involved in investigating a world I
never believed in.

It started when I received a note.

REVEREND CLARK

PLEASE VISIT MRS RUTH DAVIES IN
COVENTRY AND INVESTIGATE REPORTS OF
HAUNTING AND MISSING PERSONS.

ADDRESS ENCLOSED

Even with my unusual remit, it was a strange summons –
to debunk reported paranormal phenomena. Still, I dutifully
drove to the ancient city to seek out the address I had been
given. It was in an area called Keresley, a village which lies on
the northernmost side of Coventry.

I approached a peeling, red-painted wooden front door
and rapped politely. It was answered by a middle-aged woman
in a flour-covered apron. There were tired rings around her eyes.
While her auburn, permed hair was almost certainly well
maintained on most days, today it showed few signs of care.

"Mrs Ruth Davies?" I inquired gently.

She greeted me warmly, with a desperate hope in her voice. "Excuse the mess. I've been doing some baking to keep my mind off things," she explained as she led me to the sofa with a china cup of tea in her hands.

"It started a few weeks ago," Ruth began. "We assumed it was a prowler at first; just a hooded figure at the end of the garden. The figure came back again and again, but every time we went out to look for it, it had disappeared."

I nodded as I studied the room carefully. My eye rested upon pictures of the couple and families, and a curious old photograph of a group of men in dirty overalls, each wearing a mining helmet and smiling as they leant against a metal cart and held up ice creams in a genial salute.

"The night before last..." Ruth stopped to wipe a tear from her eye. "We saw the figure standing in the centre of the garden. Philip rushed outside to give them a good talking to. He had a terrible temper with trespassers. Twice we've been burgled in the last year and I was worried that if Philip caught them he might do them a mischief. But the hooded figure had vanished. This happened a few times and every time Philip moved quicker but couldn't see anything."

Ruth swallowed and took a sip from the cup of tea in front of her to steady her nerves. "So, when Philip saw it again he ran into the garden. It had stopped at the end, very still. Philip turned slowly to look at me and all of a sudden he had a look of absolute terror on his face. For a moment, he was bathed in a red light which seemed to come from under him, and then the ground swallowed him up and the light vanished along with him. It was like the stories we were told as children: of the ground opening and the Devil taking the souls of those who misbehaved. I ran into the darkness to see where he had gone but I couldn't find anything – not a trace of him.

"I reported it to the police but they didn't pay much heed. They were even more useless than when we tried to report the burglaries. They came out and had a look, but I think they thought I was making it up."

She gulped more tea down, trying not to spill any, although her hands were shaking. "Last night, I saw the hooded figure again. I was standing at the window and it was in the garden looking up at me. It... stared for a long time and then pointed at the ground where Philip disappeared. I think it was threatening me."

Ruth stopped and put her cup down on the table. "Reverend," she said, a sudden firmness in her voice, "I want to know if the Devil took my husband. I want to know if you can bring him back. I don't care what he did to deserve this..." Her voice faltered a little as she pleaded, "I just want him back."

I was trying hard to avoid looking sceptical in the presence of this woman's obvious pain. I couldn't agree with such extreme reasoning, but I assumed that grief and shock had its part to play in her assessment of the situation. In spite of my acceptance of the reality of a supernatural God, it seems to me that He has created a rational world and that all things have an ordered place within it.

I gave her the most reassuring smile I could and said, "I can't make any promises, Mrs Davies. But I will try to find out what happened to your husband."

I returned to my car to search through the mess of handy, practical items I keep in the boot. I took a length of rope and wooden stakes and returned to the house, through the hallway and over the linoleum-floored kitchen to the back door. Through this, I made a quiet exit into the garden of Mrs Ruth Davies.

In spite of my disbelief of Mrs Davies' story, I set myself to the task of exploring the scene. If I believe anything, it is that when someone tells you that they've seen something incredible, it is better to spend your time looking for an explanation than trying to discount their testimony.

As a precaution, I drove the wooden stakes into the ground and tied one end of the rope securely to these and the other carefully around my waist. If the Devil chose to pull my soul under, could a rope help me climb back? With this wry thought, I began walking around the garden, studying the ground.

As I tried to step through one of the denser bushes, the ground beneath me gave way and I felt myself falling. I grabbed for the rope but could not get a firm grip and gave in to the inevitability of falling; I felt a sharp pull as the rope went tight on the stakes in the ground above.

I realised I could now see around me. I was in some sort of chamber – naturally formed, with loose earth all around me. Very little light was coming into the passage through the hole above, which had mostly closed over my head, but as my eyes adjusted it was enough for me to see some details. The patch of ground I had fallen through was held together by the tangled roots of plants. They somehow had an elastic quality, which formed an almost perfect trapdoor. That was, at least, one mystery solved.

I managed to turn and take a look around me. With sadness, I saw an adult male figure lying on the bottom. His neck was grotesquely twisted and I guessed that his death must have been instant upon falling. From what little I could see, it seemed clear that this was the same Philip Davies from the cherished photos in the living room.

Mentally searching for an explanation, I recalled that this area had been heavily mined for decades. It seemed likely that undermining in the area had caused subsidence, which had opened up this cavern above a collapsed tunnel somewhere.

With great effort, I shimmied back up the rope, forced the hole back open and climbed out onto more solid earth. I lay panting on the grass for a moment, but, mindful of the open chamber below me, I quickly moved to a part of the garden I believed would be more firm.

I broke the news to Mrs Davies before I left. I think people imagine that priests develop a resistance for breaking this kind of news – but I can assure you that it is never nice to give or to receive this manner of tidings. I stayed with her for as long as she needed and I left her with details of local bereavement counselling services.

Returning to my car, I found a handwritten note. Oddly, it was not tucked under the wipers as one would expect. The wind was holding it in place against the glass on the driver window – something which the note's author could surely not have relied upon?

The note began "TO THE PRIEST" and gave directions through nearby streets to some wasteland between Keresley and the nearby M6 motorway. Curious, yet very guardedly, I followed these directions until I had to abandon my car at a point where I found I had to proceed on foot.

The instructions led me almost perfectly to another opening in the ground. I returned to the car and fetched a powerful torch in order to have a good look inside.

Stashed in the hole were crates of beer, scattered takeaway trays and an assortment of televisions, car stereos, videogame consoles and jewellery boxes. I'd stumbled upon a burglar's stash!

Carefully, I stepped down the short ladder that had been placed against the edge of the opening and looked around. This passage was evidence of more subsidence. For some reason, instead of caving in completely, the earth had split and formed a natural passage. There was a tunnel leading away from the opening. I gathered my bearings and realised that the passage must head towards the estate on which Mrs Davies lived.

I followed it for a short way but soon came to a dead end – a complete cave-in. As I was about to turn, my foot caught something. I looked down and saw a boot, sticking eerily out of the soil.

The police came and cleared the scene. The body belonged to a local kid who had gone missing. His name was Ryan Morris and he was a local thief. He must have been using the tunnel to get in and out without being seen during his nocturnal activities. Associates stated that he always wore a hooded top.

My satisfaction at realising that this accounted for the Davies' hooded figure receded when I was told that Ryan had been dead for several weeks. Furthermore, the section of the tunnel he was in had been deliberately collapsed using a trip wire and mining charges.

I felt myself go cold. The police said they were looking for "Someone with hard feelings towards a local thief; someone with knowledge of mining and possibly demolition".

I remembered the picture I had studied in Ruth's living room: Philip Davies standing smiling with his old mining crew. He could have discovered the tunnel Ryan was using to conduct his burglaries and built a trap out of old mining equipment. I considered the possible irony that it may have been the demolition of the tunnel that caused the instability in his own garden. Killed by his own trap?

My moral dilemma was whether to tell anybody what I found out. Ryan was dead; Davies was dead. Did causing a widow to suffer the sullying of her husband's name outweigh the need for Ryan's family to know his fate? I didn't know.

Plus, there was the unresolved issue: if Ryan had died weeks before, who had the Davies been seeing in their garden?

At that point, I still doubted the existence of ghosts; but I had read that some believe that the spirits of murder victims reveal themselves to make evident the truth of their deaths. Maybe, in the end, that was why I did eventually choose to reveal my findings, to Ruth and to the police. I still don't know if any of them believed me.

Yet, if I needed any kind of reward for a thankless job, perhaps it came when I returned home and noticed something in my rear-view mirror before I got out of my car. Lying on the back seat was a muddied hoodie, to which was stuck a crumpled note, which simply read:

THANK YOU

To shirley , George all the best!

A Message to You

Ian Collier

Dear Coventry Cat Woman

I have to write. I am sure you're not a bad person; a bad person would have thrown Lola under a car or hit her. I know why you put her in the bin. Most people understand it, but they are trying to pretend they don't. We all often have *Dark Thoughts*. Everyone. I can't look over the balcony of the top floor of the West Orchards. At least I can't without wondering what it would be like to see the floors rushing upwards. Would I land headfirst and end it in a blink or would I find myself lying unable to move, apart from my eyes? My eyes gazing up to the worried eyes of strangers peering down at my body. Why would they be worried? Worried for a stranger; someone they don't know? Would they just be peeping, like Tom, to see something they aren't meant to? Probably worried that someday their demons will overcome them!

I can't talk about it with people, not any longer. When I tried, they told me I was mad, but there was recognition.

"Stop your messing around," they said.

You can't tell me that we are the only two people who get these thoughts – the ideas that spring up out of nowhere that we should do things. I remember wanting to shout out during the school Christmas service that Mr Levi was the Antichrist. I always resisted; one year I bit my lip so hard that I started to bleed. I ran from the church, blood and saliva dribbling down my chin. As I ran from the church, I crashed into him outside of the door.

If he wasn't the Antichrist, why wasn't he inside with the rest of us?

Don't trust teachers or the doctors.

Rudy

Pilgrims

Martin Brown

I met a band of pilgrims
In town the other day.
They told me they had travelled
From very far away.

"What brings you here to Coventry?"
I asked of them, in wonder,
And when they gave their reason
I realised their blunder.

"We came because we heard about
Your many holy roads!
We gathered from the news reports
That you have loads and loads!"

I had to smile as I explained
To these deluded souls,
That Coventry's roads aren't holy –
They're merely full of holes!

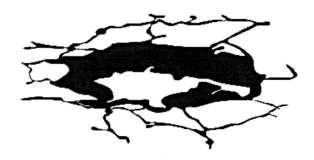

A Question of Tears

Calvin Hedley

"Why's that man crying, Mummy?"

I spent the night of the November blitz in a public shelter on the Foleshill Road. Having visited Aunty Bet and Uncle Frank that Thursday, my parents and I were making our way back to Lord Street, Chapelfields, when the sirens began. It was beautifully clear, with a bright 'bomber's moon', but we had no conception of the hammer blow that was about to descend.

Coventry had witnessed a few nuisance raids, but myths of immunity still circulated: the city nestled in a valley and would escape detection, or Coventry was too far for enemy bombers to carry sufficient bomb loads. These were commonly held misconceptions that in many ways kept the war at a distance.

It seems almost incredible now, but at the time it was the most natural thing in the world for schoolboys, having evaded the watchfulness of parents, to roam the streets once the sirens had sounded, seeking that most prized of possessions, the altitude fusing mechanism from German bombs. These were complicated devices fashioned from shiny brass, and their fascinating appeal more than offset any perceived danger. Besides, hardly anything had happened before, and the darkened streets, probing searchlights and surging sirens represented a fantastic opportunity for adventure.

There was no chance to escape on this occasion, as we hurried to seek safety.

I stood outside the shelter, gazing towards the town, and it soon became clear that something new was at hand. Chandelier flares intensified the moonlight and the drone of aeroplanes swelled the air – not the steady monotone of British aircraft but a throbbing, resonant beat that somehow sounded out of kilter. It was all happening so quickly. Incendiary baskets began to fall, shedding their deadly sticklets to the winds. I was transfixed. The incendiaries burned with an unnatural intensity, producing a brilliant blue-white glare. They started many small fires, but only when the high explosives began to fall did the sky deepen to a vivid carmine red, shot through with purple, pink and orange close to the rooftops. The town, with its narrow, cobbled streets and many half-timbered buildings, was being incinerated. I scampered into the shelter.

All night they came shrieking down like maddened banshees. The ground shuddered continually and, occasionally, hot air blasts would rush in on us, like heavy blows that made my eardrums ache and seared my nostrils. The landmines were utterly terrifying. They exploded with a kind of C-R-U-M-P and the ground itself seemed to wince. I began to cry bitterly and clung to my mother until my muscles ached.

Always the sound of bombs, clanging fire bells, pounding anti-aircraft fire, yapping dogs … and people – people shouting, screaming, dying. The smells were choking; burning timbers, brick and plaster dust, gas and spent explosives filled the shelter. I grew too tired or scared to cry, and withstood the mayhem like a cringing rabbit, cowering under my mother's coat.

It was morning before the bombs stopped. There was no all-clear sounded, but we eventually emerged at about seven-thirty – numbed and shaken, but thankful. A slight drizzle, sullied by the smoke, melted to nothing on the scorching city. Fires blazed all around, casting blackened ash petals, like macabre confetti, high into the air. The water mains were ruptured, so many fires were simply left to burn themselves out. We learned a few days later that many people sheltering in a

Broadgate cellar could not escape from leaking mains water and were all drowned.

Some policemen were trying to corner a horse that careered about in crazed terror. It stumbled on some rubble not far from us and its legs flayed wildly to regain purchase. It whinnied ceaselessly.

We tried to return to Uncle Frank's, only to be barred by cordons, unexploded bombs and the utter mess. So we headed into the centre – concerned, confused and uncertain. We never saw our relatives again. They had gone to a neighbour's Anderson shelter, but it had received a direct hit.

That journey home was a crazy mix of terrible destruction, surreal imagery and abject tragedy. Debris was everywhere. Smoke swathed the city in mournful garb. Lampposts and telegraph poles leant at strange angles. A burst gas main sent a jet of fire, blue at the base, with a flourishing yellow plume, high above the houses. Shredded blackout material hung from windows. There were houses without roofs, or with walls blown out, or there was just rubble. Craters pockmarked the streets and the tram system never recovered. Its overhead cables lay across the roads – nobody knew whether they still carried a charge – while the tramlines themselves were mangled, sometimes standing erect like giant liquorice sticks. Glass crunched with every step.

And so we walked, clambered and crawled our way to the city centre. The devastation became more terrible as we neared the town. Pool Meadow was badly mauled and the nearby sawmill and Triumph motorcycle factory were burning. We could see the old Market Tower and the spires of Holy Trinity, Christ Church and the cathedral – charred fingers pointing accusingly at the smoke-filled sky.

Soldiers were combing some flattened wasteland, putting things into potato sacks. My father hurried us on, and it only dawned on me when passing the Gaumont cinema that the troops were collecting human remains.

We stumbled on. Fragmented images come to mind: the foul stink of gas, the Council House with all its windows out, a car in a crater down Little Park Street, the hot, singeing air, greedy, crackling fires and the cathedral, burning to our right, a heart-rending microcosm of Coventry's plight. I was thirteen years old and had never heard of Dante's *Inferno*, but if I had, this would have been the overriding essence of my impressions: a hellish, broiling nightmare. It was simply impossible to avoid strange and shocking images, wherever you looked.

Martins Bank in the High Street sported a large union flag, suspended from a horizontal flagpole – a bright patch of defiant colour amidst the soot and smoke. The National Provincial Bank had also escaped, complete with its distinctive front steps and columns. Owen Owens, Burtons and many other shops in Broadgate were less fortunate and blazed fiercely. The Keresley bus was marooned there, a burnt-out husk with its tyres and windows gone.

Along Hertford Street, the Empire Theatre and Queen's Hotel were on fire, and there were smouldering heaps of rubble to negotiate. Bull Yard's shelter had caved in, its concrete roof crushing those inside. A man in a ragged, torn suit stood nearby. His arms hung limply, one hand crushing a dark-brown hat. Streaming tears left pale streaks down his sooted face – a minute drop of suffering lost in the common sump of the city's misery.

A family was passing and a small child asked, "Why's that man crying, Mummy?"

The destruction became patchier again nearer home and we began to believe that our house had survived. We were very lucky. Most of the windows and roofing tiles had gone, but the house stood. Down the road were three houses with only their fronts remaining. There was no gas, water or electricity, but we were home and had survived.

Over the next few days, a sorry stream of bombed-out people trudged up Hearsall Lane. I had seen newsreels of European refugees on the move, pushing, dragging or carrying all that they possessed. And now the scene was before me in stained colour. Prams, weird trolleys, carts and laden wretches moved by in a sullen, scowling silence. I could only imagine where they headed – out of the city, presumably, but Coventry was sealed off. Morbid sightseers and concerned relatives were prevented from entering by the authorities. There was also some looting, but I suppose adversity will bring out the best and worst in people.

Some of the fires still burned after Christmas, and the charred smell lingered for months. The war receded from Coventry for a while (there were no big raids until the following Easter), but it was a hard road back to anything like normality. Rationing was increased, my father turned in at the Standard factory that Monday, and trips to the local bakery held perils from unexploded bombs. Even the playground trade in bomb detritus, previously sporadic with yearned-for mechanisms or shrapnel, suddenly seemed pointless. Everyone already seemed to have something. We mourned our loss.

The events of that night cast a long, long shadow and recovery was slow, but in those savage times it was survival that counted. In truth, I've probably suffered more, considering such memories in later life, than I did as a schoolboy, but then, time is a great teacher as well as healer. One day, we may come to learn the lesson fully.

A Coventry Tale

Sarah Boxwell
Age 10

As
the bombs
fell over
Coventry and
the old cathedral,
Children went somewhere safer
because of the bombs.
As I walk across
Coventry now,
all I see of the
old cathedral is ruins.
I remember the history
of the old cathedral
now in ruins.
Dear old Coventry
What a state the old cathedral is in!
Goodbye old cathedral.
You stood tall
You were brave.

Remembrance

Mary Ogilvie

There was a mist to the evening air,
Passers-by were few,
As dotted about here and there
They carried on about their business.
Light artificial in the making,
Cast its glare here and there
On buildings within its view.

The two men's steps were heavy, slow and definite.
Time was filling in its pages between them
As they walked in silent agreement,
Bitten only by conversation caught up on yester-year.
The space between them was thin,
And shoulders high but straight in woollen coats met
As their steps took them upwards, onwards,
Above ancient steps to a visible stage before them.

The stage was set, the players had long since taken their bow.
The air was light, but full and steeped with the ages.
A floodlight cast eerie shadows
Into corners and places on faces half eaten,
But yet held features bearing strength
And glared on those who stared upon them.

Long ago all was new,
But battering rains and storms have loosened stone,
And that freshest hold lost,
Now appears rugged at its sharpest point.
The floor now worn by heel of shoe ups and bends,
And cuts across and down,
As moss grows in cracks and corners hidden,
But yet visible to the human eye.
Does it tell its age they wonder,
But yet mystery holds its splendour,
And the naked images although pitiful to their maker,
Hold that glamour in reserve,
For age had added its tale of experience.

Their mantle stone in colour, still holds their note of existence,
And respect which is duly theirs is given by the onlooker
Although curiosity is sometimes in the making.
The old and new mingle together,
But yet by time so much apart,
Has progression really shown the way,
Or is its image portraying fact from fantasy?
All around is laid out the images from the past.
Do they indulge feeling or other monuments
To add to the glory of the past?

A cold wind blows silently around the tomb,
And the glare of the lights does nothing to warm the onlookers.
Pulling collar over neck, their hands thrust into pocket,
They slowly descend,
As the chimes ring out their duty
In a space of short time, but yet of long ago,
The two men slowly walked away.

The Stuff of Daydreams

Derek Medcraft

They had just finished dinner; it was Sunday. The children knew it was Sunday because Dad and Jamie had retired to the parlour room. They were only allowed in the parlour on Sundays or if someone important like the priest visited. And at Christmas, of course.

Mum and Maggie cleared the plates away and washed up as the kettle boiled.

"Dad, can you read the letter again, please?" said Jamie.

"Okay," said Jim. "We'll wait until your mother and Maggie join us. They won't be long."

"Bridget, when you come in with the tea, can you bring the letter with you, please?" shouted Jim into the other room, which doubled as a kitchen, dining and living room.

"Which letter would that be?" said Bridget, knowingly teasing Jim. They only had one in the last two years and that was to remind them they were behind on the rent.

Bridget gave Jim the letter as she and Maggie joined father and son in the parlour. "You'll wear that letter out, the way you keep reading it!" said Bridget.

Maggie chuckled as only a ten-year-old does at silly jokes.

Jim carefully retrieved the pages from the envelope and began to read, including the address in the top right-hand corner.

22 Coundon Road,
Coundon,
Coventry

12th May 1932

Dear Jim,

It was a long and tiring journey down to
Coventry on the bus, but quite surprising. I saw
more countryside and towns than I ever believed
existed in England. It took ten hours, bouncing
around in an old jalopy. I reckon old Moses' pony
and trap would have been quicker and there were
three changes of bus too. But I'm here now and
have been for four weeks.

The first lodgings I stayed at were not very
good, so I only stayed there for a week, and then
a friend at work recommended this place. That's
the address at the top.

It's a huge house, there are three floors
with four bedrooms on each floor except for the
ground floor and there are some rooms in the
attic although Mrs Brannigan will only let them
for a short time if someone is of good character,
highly recommended and needy. And what's more,
you won't believe this, each floor has a room with
a toilet and a bath in, and the bath has hot and
cold running water. No more sitting in the old tin

tub in front of the fire while the kids have to play outside.

For this luxury –

"What's hot and cold running water, Mum?" asked Maggie.

"It's the stuff of daydreams," said Bridget. "Now let your dad finish reading the letter. Again."

They all laughed.

For this luxury Mrs Brannigan charges £5 10s 00d for your own room or £3 2s 00d if are you are prepared to share. I'm sharing a room but you ought to see it, it's huge. You could get six of us Tuckers in this room, and there's carpet on the floor too. And you get breakfast and dinner each day and for an extra two shillings a week, Mrs Brannigan will do you sandwiches for work.

There's loads of jobs down here in the car factories. I'm at the Standard. They say one day every house will have a car, can you believe it?

Also if you save a bit of money and are in regular employment you can get a mortgage and –

"What's a mor – ?"

"Hush, Jamie, let your dad finish reading," said Bridget.

... and buy your own house with hot and cold running water and a garden.

Can you imagine us Tuckers with our own houses, with gardens and a car to boot? Jim, you've got to come down and see this.

Last Saturday afternoon I walked to the town centre. Do you remember old Cleggy the history teacher and how he used to talk about those medieval buildings? Well it's just like that. The streets are narrow and cobble stoned, the buildings are those ones with the wooden beams showing and the top of the building is bigger than the bottom. I'm sure if you leant out the top window you could shake hands with the person in the building opposite.

Don't wait any longer, Jim, come down here now. I've already had a word with Mrs Brannigan and she can put you up for a short time.

I've enclosed a postal order for three shillings. Take it to the post office counter, hand it over and they will give you three shillings. Get Bridget something nice, buy yourself a couple of beers and get some sweets for the kids.

I'll write again soon.

Billy

"What do you reckon, Bridget?" asked Jim.

"It's the stuff of daydreams, but Billy always did make things sound better than they are. Anyways, all our family and friends are here."

Just then, the house trembled, as did all the houses in that terrace and every other terrace in the town. There was a rumble emanating from deep within the ground. The few ornaments they had on the mantelpiece trembled.

Bridget's face went ashen. She and Jim had experienced this too many times before. They knew they would be joining the town in a vigil at the pithead, waiting for them to bring the dead husbands, sons and brothers out of the pit. Well, the ones they could get at.

Jim rose from the chair. "I'll get my work clothes on. They're going to need me."

As Jim made his way upstairs there was loud, anxious knocking on the front door. Bridget answered it.

"There's been an accident at the pit," said Mrs McPherson.

"We gathered," said Bridget. "Jim will be there shortly."

Jim came down the stairs, dressed ready to join the mine rescue team. As he reached the door, Bridget threw her arms around his neck and whispered in his ear, "Be careful."

Just as he was going through the door, Bridget said, "I'll have your best shirt and your suit ironed and ready for when you come back. You'll need that if you're going to go for an interview."

Jim looked at Bridget and the kids, smiled and winked before he set off for the pithead. He could already see dust pouring skywards from the lift shaft.

"Are we going to Coventry?" asked Jamie.

The Horse's Tale

Martin Brown

"And what was it like?" asked the duck with a quack,
"To have a nude lady, astride, on your back?"
"Were her buttocks all soft? Could you feel her behind?"
continued the duck with the singular mind.
"Were you nervous?" interrupted the cow, with a moo,
"To think everyone might be staring at you?"
"None dared to look!" neighed the horse, with aplomb,
"Except one nosy rascal; chap's name was Tom:
And me and my Lady were the last things he saw.
Struck down by our Lord! – Now he'll see no more!"
"A load of old rubbish!" said the frog, with a croak;
"Her ladyship, naked? Come on, it's a joke!
I never believe such tales without proof…"

At this provocation, the horse hit the roof:
"You yokels know nothing! – except about farms!
I have been privy to her Ladyship's charms!
I was her favourite; it was me that she chose
To ride on that day, without any clothes!
And what a day! So sunny and bright!
The streets were deserted, all kept out of sight.
We rode through the town, aloof, without fear,
'til a large rat ran out, and caused me to rear.
I threw off my Lady, she fell in the mud;
No bones were broken, she didn't draw blood.
She quickly remounted, we set off once more.

No one had seen us, of that I'm quite sure.
Nothing was said, and no one was told...
But the very next day, I was led off and sold,
and ended up here, in this grotty place;
I've come down in the world, but can still cut a pace!"

And with that, he trotted, down the old, muddy track,
so the others could gossip, behind his proud back.
"A load of old tosh! I'll not heed a word!"
"From beginning to end, the story's absurd!"
"The nag's going senile; his memory plays tricks –
He loves telling lies! He does it for kicks!"
"He's made it all up! It's a load of old guff!
Only humans believe in that sort of stuff!"

And with that, the animals all went their own ways,
and did what they must, to fill out their days.
And day followed day, as the years took their course,
and no one paid heed to a silly old horse.
And when the horse finally drew his last breath
none mourned his passing, in a world full of death.
But with his demise went the last chance to know
if his memories were real, or just dreams, long ago.

Ghost Town

Ian Collier

Author's Note:

The Foleshill Road complex was founded as a textile Spinning Mill by Samuel Courtauld and Company Limited in 1904. It was opened in 1905, spinning small quantities of Viscose yarn, and was the first mill in the world to spin this commercially. By 1910, when the building now called Tower Court, was added, output had reached 10 tonnes a week and 2,000 people worked there. Tower Court won a design award in 2001, after it had been refurbished as office space.

I work in Tower Court. It used to be a textile mill; now it's offices and a call centre. I wear a headset, a springy piece of steel that clamps an earphone to each side of my head. From one of the earphones, a mouthpiece protrudes to arc around my cheek. Its extension, as it stretches around my face, can be adjusted by a slight pressure pulling or pushing along its telescopic arm, and the positioning of the earpieces on the steel arch can also be adjusted by sliding them along the horseshoe of metal. The headset will work equally well for any size of head. When people start work here, they are loaned a newly cleaned headset; should their employment terminate for any reason, the payment of their final week's wage is dependent upon the return of an undamaged headset. That is their headset for the duration of their work in the call centre or until wear renders it in need of replacement.

I am in my fifth month of working here. By call centre standards, I am now an old hand, but not of sufficient longevity to be considered for a team leader's position. That avenue for promotion will become accessible to me in three weeks' time, should I wish to set my foot upon the corporate ladder. I regularly have new employees placed with me so they can "get a feel for the job". Some will survive the first three days and be given their own headset to cherish.

There are many temporary jobs in today's economy and I have tried most of them. My forearms still bear the weals inflicted by cookers in fast food establishments and I recall the hours of shelf filling as a replenishment technician. I have also picked orders in a warehouse, presumably as a deplenishment associate.

I enjoy the relative freedom of dress that the call centre affords one: no corporate tee shirt, no name badge; however, I feel that this is the ultimate in transitory working. The closest thing to a reference point is your headset. We "hot-desk": that means we grab the first available seat at our team's station. The team's station drifts, depending on which teams are working what shift.

The hours change weekly as shift patterns demand. The shift patterns can change diurnally, especially for someone like me, depending on the requirements of new people needing training and regular staff calling in sick. If one changes from one's expected shift, they change teams, too. It is now twelve days since I last worked with my team and I am currently working with my second team since then.

The next closest thing to a reference point is the "customer welcome script". The headset rings. You are expected to press a button on your modem to take the call before the third buzz. The skin on the pad of my index finger slides over the surface of the switch. I can feel every groove in the triangle design that is embossed in the plastic. My manicured nail starts to flex as pressure is applied and then, in an instant, contact is made. I'm live again.

"Hello/ Good morning/ Good evening – you are through to the XXXXX service, I am Charles and your name is?"

Customer responds

"And how can I help you today, Mr I-just-want-to-get-this-sodding-thing-done?"

Customer responds

"What sort of card will you be paying with, Mr I-just-want…?"

Customer responds

"Could you read the long number on the cruddy card, Mr I-just-want…?"

Customer responds

"Thank you, sir, and what is the expiry date on your sodding card, Mr I-just-want…?"

Customer responds

"Thank you, and what are the last three digits of the security code from the back of your sodding card, Mr I-just-want…?"

Customer responds

I dream that I can improvise.

"Thank you, sir, I am about to take the £17 and 15 pence from your account, Mr I-just-want… do you authorise that payment?"

Customer responds

"Yes sir, the basic cost is only £2, but our terms clearly state that there is a 15 pence charge for paying by card and –"

Customer interrupts

"We accept all major credit and debit cards so, yes, you could pay from your naff west account by debit card. That, too, would incur the 15 pence fee.

Customer responds

"I'm sorry, sir, we can't take cash or cheques." I keep going. "There is also £1 swear-charge for any vulgarities used in such a way as to offend our staff. You total bill is now £23.15."

Customer interrupts

"That will now be £33 and 15 pence... and yes, sir, you are correct. I should point out that, although you do technically have a choice over payment, failing to acquire authorisation on the day will result in a £70 fine plus the swear-charge and a 100% surcharge on the swear-charge. Of course, I would have to deduct that full amount from your account should you hang up the phone."

Today I am working a late shift. I see most of my teammates as I arrive and they leave. I am starting work at 6pm – I have to be plugged into my console and logged into my computer before 5.55 to ensure that everything is functioning correctly. I wave to my teammates as they finish their last calls, some unable to extricate themselves until after 6.20. They are, however, only paid for working until 6pm.

I am left alone today at this station as everyone drifts off home. As time passes, the 12–7 workers gradually clear out, leaving the late shift stranded like a few surviving humans in a post-apocalyptic world, disjointed and both hoping not to be alone, yet wishing to remain isolated. I have been allocated my evening break times for the whole night.

It is now 20:00 hours and I can take a half-hour meal break. I eat a pasty, warm from the microwave. The filling is powdery and has sinews of what I hope is vegetable matter, the chunks of potato. These are listed as part of the filling, though the product is not marketed as a potato, onion and cheese-flavourings E621 and E635 pasty. I rinse it down with a vending machine hot chocolate that is marginally less foul than the coffee or tea. I visit the toilet and am back to my headset by

20:29. I now have to wait two hours before my next break. That will last for fifteen minutes and during it, I will smoke one roll-up, visit the toilet and get a cup of water from the cooler.

It is now 22:34. I took a call at 22:28. My break will be over in 11 minutes' time. I decide that I can make it through the rest of the shift without a visit to the toilet. In an alcove outside the fire exit, I inhale deeply and drag the smoke into my lungs. The night air is cold; the drunken shouts and screeching traffic are loud against the sound of a city that is otherwise turning in for the night. The stress and frustration stemming from the rudeness of "customers" is smeared and suffocated under a film of tar and nicotine.

I blow long slow plumes that obscure the stars, then I remember the nightmare that awaits. I glance at my watch and dash back through the fire exit, racing up the steps two at a time, around the corners as they wind around the lift shaft, three flights between each floor, like a squared-off spiral staircase. I pass the teak-effect doors with the glass portholes on the first floor. I continue to race up, and pass identical doors on the second.

As I start on the final flight of stairs, I look up at yet another identical pair of doors, then I stumble and fall. I feel the bang on my head starting to swell almost before I stand up. I am unsteady on my feet. I stumble backwards and the world spins as I slump back against the wall. I know that I need to make it out of the stairwell; no one will come this way again till mid-morning, so passing out here wouldn't be good.

I gaze at the red bricks of the outside of the lift shaft... I would have sworn they were painted grey. I hear the tittering of girls. What are they doing here at this time? Next, the smell hits me... ammonia and a smell like igniting matches combine to make my head spin anew.

"Oi! Come on, Charlie, stop acting such a gobbin," laughs one of the girls. "I reckon you've been watching too many Music Hall drunks."

Her friend adds, with less of a laugh in her voice. "It's all right for the likes of you; some of us are on piece work, you know."

I manage to grunt. I look up at them again; I see huge incandescent bulbs forming halos behind the girls. The one with the big eyes strikes me as beautiful. I am unsure why, but something doesn't quite look right...

The words 'diffuser' and 'suspended ceiling' spring to mind, but I'm not quite sure what they mean.

"Edna, I don't think he's clowning around. Charlie? Do you know where you are, duck?" says the big-eyed girl.

"By heck, he really does look confused, don't he, Mavis? An' look at that egg swelling up."

Edna and Mavis come down towards me. I try to wave them away but I nearly fall down the flight of stairs to my left. I grab the handrail to steady myself as each of them takes me by an arm and helps me to the top of the flight. Mavis's hand brushes against mine. This is the third floor and there's a big white '3' painted in a black square on the bare wall – this is where I am headed. Why?

They help me through the heavy rubber doors, which slap back on themselves as we enter a world of noise – the smell is nauseating now.

We walk across the shop floor. I look down the rows of spinning frames. I notice the glass covers of one are open, as though the acid cakes are ready for doffing, but no one is there to doff them. Then I remember I was supposed to be fixing its godets for Mavis. She sent a message down to say they were working loose again.

As they lead me out through the doors on the other side of the shop floor and into the tearoom, Edna says, "It looks like your loom's stopped for the rest of the shift. Should I tell the overlooker?"

"Aye, if you don't mind. You can leave us alone; I'll make him a brew. He'll soon be right as rain."

As Edna leaves, I ask. "Mavis, I know it's a fanciful question, but how long have I worked here?"

"Well duck, you were here when I started two years ago, but all the time I've known you you've always been threatening to get a job at the car works. I'm not sure if you'd put them off with your posh talk, though. 'Fanciful' indeed..."

I glance at my hands. They are rough, with ingrained oil and dirt.

Then she sticks her head out of the door and glances around outside, before drawing back into the tearoom.

She bends down and kisses me on the mouth. "I hope we're still set for the Hippodrome tomorrow night. I'd be right upset if you were trying to get out of our date."

"Oh no, certainly not, but you'll have to remind me of the details."

She smiles and kisses me again.

I feel a surge of electricity in my heart and a mule kick to my chest.

I say, "I'd rather die than miss our date."

Past Participants

Gareth Layzell

November 22, 1963

Benny hesitated with his key in the door. He was shaking, as he always was on days like this. On days like this, he was reminded of how his life had been. It wasn't that he was unhappy with his life now, far from it, but on days like this it was harder to forget what he had lost. And today... today was the worst one so far. Possibly the worst he and Emma would have to face. He glanced briefly over his shoulder at the spires on the skyline, taking comfort in their presence, then turned the key and pushed the door open.

Bernadette appeared from nowhere as soon as he was through the door and flung her arms around him. "Daddy! It's horrible."

She didn't cry – Bernadette seldom did – but she was shaking almost as much as he had been outside. She was the youngest, but at eleven she was old enough to grasp the enormity of what had happened.

"I know," he said, hugging her and ruffling her hair gently. "I know." Keeping one arm around her, he dropped his walking stick into the coat stand, then stepped into the living room.

Cath was sitting on the floor, in her favourite spot by his armchair, hugging her knees. Christopher, the eldest, was on the settee, staring into space. Benny's wife Emma was sitting next to Christopher, but she stood up as soon as Benny entered the room and kissed him.

"They announced the news at the station," he said solemnly.

"We already had the telly on," Emma replied. "We're just waiting to see what else they can tell us."

Benny could see so many unspoken words in her eyes. Words that he wanted to say, too, but that the children were not ready to hear. Those words would have to wait until later.

He looked around, allowing himself to see and hear the television for the first time. That was when he noticed that there was nothing to hear. The picture was just the BBC's trademark revolving globe.

"Turn it off," he said. "There's nothing more they can tell us. Kennedy is dead. What more do we need to know?"

"Don't we need to know why? Or who?" Christopher asked. "What if it was the Russians, because of what happened in Cuba, or something?"

Benny opened his mouth to say, "It wasn't the Russians," but then caught himself and stopped. Even though he was used to guarding what he said, it didn't get any easier. "It doesn't matter who or why right now," he said. "It just is."

Christopher looked up at him, and Benny could see how scared his son was. He wished he could say something more reassuring, something that wouldn't lead to questions that neither he nor Emma were ready for just yet. And then he found it. "I don't think the Russians would be that stupid," he said. "If they were, they'd never have backed down in Cuba."

"You think so?" Christopher asked. The boy stopped and thought about this, then nodded. "Maybe you're right."

Benny looked back up at Emma. "Reg will be on his way here. You know what he's like."

"Dad?" Cath asked. "Why does Uncle Reg always come to visit when something bad happens? He always wants to talk to you about it. It's very odd."

Benny smiled. This wasn't quite one of the questions he wasn't ready for yet, but it was close. Still, he couldn't help but be impressed that Cath had noticed. They'd always done their best to play things down, but it was bound to have come up sooner or later. It wasn't much of a surprise that it had been Cath who had spoken up first. Christopher was very much about the big picture; it was Cath who always noticed the small details.

"It's just his way," was all Benny could manage in reply.

It was another half hour before there was a knock at the door. Emma went to answer it. Benny had taken up residence in his armchair by then, and with the war wound in his leg still aching from the walk home, it was difficult to get up.

He hesitated before looking up as Reg entered the room. He was never quite sure what emotion he'd see in his friend's eyes on these occasions, although it was a fair bet that he wouldn't like it.

Reg stopped briefly in the living room doorway and stared at Benny. While Reg's bushy moustache and clothes were as immaculate as ever, his demeanour conveyed a sense of dishevelled exhaustion. The look in his eyes was one of betrayal. That was new to Benny. He'd seen fear and anger before, but never had his friend looked at him as if what had happened was his fault.

"Hello, Benny," Reg said, his voice faltering a little.

"Hello, Reg," Benny said in a flat voice. "Good to see you."

Emma looked around at the children nervously. "I'll make a pot of tea," she said. "Children, upstairs please. Benny and Uncle Reg need to talk. It'll soon be bedtime, anyway."

The three children left the room quickly and without protest, not needing to be told twice. Emma closed the door behind them before heading through the other door into the kitchen.

"You knew!" Reg hissed. "Something like this, and you knew!"

"Of course I knew," Benny replied with a catch in his voice. "Did you?"

Reg flinched visibly from the question then came back angrily. "What exactly is that supposed to mean? Are you really suggesting – ?"

Benny cut him off. "Everyone is going to have a theory about why Kennedy was shot. Every government on the planet will get blamed at some point." He waved his hand and looked down. "Don't worry, I don't seriously think Her Majesty's Government had something to do with it, but sooner or later someone will."

Reg seemed to relax a little, and he sat down on the settee. "But you knew. You could have said something." His voice was little more than a whisper.

"Would you really have believed me if I had? Or would you have thought I was seeing just how much you would believe?"

"I don't know. I really don't know."

"It kills me," Benny said, "knowing about all these things that are going to happen. Although I have to admit, this one caught me by surprise. I knew it was this year, but I had no idea when."

"I don't think this is a date anyone is going to forget in a hurry," Reg replied.

"Reg, it's 1963. I'm not due to be born for another ten years. It's already history by the time I learn about it. There are other things I do remember. Other things that aren't easy to forget. You might believe me, but your superiors? Would they believe you? We've been over this before, more than once, and you know it's true. I don't think it's possible to change what I know happens, which is why I mostly stay well away from it. I stick to my simple job and my simple life and the simple things that aren't already written... or aren't to me, at least."

Reg gave him a pained, desperate look. "Would it be so wrong to try to change things? To try and stop things like Kennedy's death?"

Benny sighed. "Say I could change it. At that point, the world I came from no longer exists. And who can say for sure that the world replacing it would be any better? Ultimately it could be a lot worse."

"This is what you always say."

"That's because I've thought this through, many many times. The other possibility is worse, for me at least. Say I try to change it, and find I can't. In doing so, I prove that history is already set in stone. In effect, I have no free will. The results of my actions are already determined, whether I like it or not. I would not like it."

"But this is already what you think. Why would knowing it be any worse? Why would trying be any worse?"

"It's what I think, and it's what I suspect, but it's not what I know. I keep myself in this simple situation because I do not know the detail of what is to come, for my family and friends, at least. Even if I don't have free will, I have the illusion of it, and I have some room to manoeuvre. I've talked to Emma about it enough to know she feels the same."

Reg's eyes lit up. Now he was intrigued. "Room to manoeuvre?"

Benny nodded. "You've asked before why I chose to live here in Coventry, even though, in the future, it'll be where I grow up. Even though at some point I could meet my own parents, or even myself. It's because 23 years ago, Coventry made me realise I had room to manoeuvre."

Reg didn't have to ask what event he was referring to. "Coventry getting bombed made you realise that? How? What did you change?"

Benny opened his mouth to speak but was interrupted by Emma bringing through a tray of tea. When they settled again, Emma was watching him as intently as Reg was. She knew the story, but she'd never heard him tell it.

"I don't know that I changed anything," Benny began. "In fact, I'm pretty sure I didn't. But it was when I realised how I could be part of history instead of just hiding from it. I knew the date the bombs would come. And, well, this city is my home. It wasn't out of some morbid fascination or anything like that, but I knew I had to see it for myself.

"I don't know exactly what I needed to see. It wasn't as if I wanted to just sit outside the city and watch the bombs fall. We hadn't meant to be that close to the city when it started. But we were. I got Emma into a shelter and then went to leave it again. A warden stopped me and asked what I thought I was doing. I just replied, 'You're going to need help.' It's one of the stupidest things I've ever done, but it's also something I'm proud of." His eyes began to sting.

"I knew that I had things to do. In the future, I saw a photo of me and Emma that was taken in 1943. So I gambled on the idea that this meant I was safe from harm. My leg wasn't so bad then. I could still move around quite quickly. I helped get people to safety, knowing somehow that I wouldn't be hurt in the process. I saved twenty-three people that night. And I had more lucky escapes than anyone would ever believe." Benny paused, wiping his eyes.

"Do you see now?" he asked. "Being in this city reminds me of that, on the days that I find this unusual life hard to cope with. It reminds me that there is still so much I can do, even if I can't change the big things."

Reg nodded. "I think I do. I don't know if I can accept it, but I think I understand. I wish you'd told me this before."

"I don't like to talk about it," Benny said. "I saved people, but I saw people die, too." He wiped his eyes again and looked down, fighting back tears. He only looked back up when he heard the creak of the door opening.

Cath stood there, her face white. In her eyes, Benny could see all the questions he'd always feared, all the questions he'd always hoped could wait for another day.

"What do you mean, you're not due to be born for another ten years?"

Tom

Derek Medcraft

Where's me plate?
In front of you
He rested his hands on the table, a yard apart
They were builder's hands, hard and gnarled
The winters were tough, but work was scarce
You took what you could, when you could
The earl had always been that way
Always had work available in the winter
When there wasn't much about
Tuppence a day. Less than normal
He was a tight bastard
He never went without his taxes though
Those at the top paid more
But they made more
Those at the bottom paid less
But they hardly scraped a living
Somebody had to pay for all their finery
He and his wife were never short
Although some say
Mainly those who work at the big house
He and his wife don't see eye to eye
He slid his hands slowly together
Across the table top
Clink, he heard where his knife and fork were
As they touched the side of his plate
Knife in right hand
Fork in left
Clenched fingers feeling the side of the plate

Wife, where's me peas said he
1 o'clock
Potatoes 4 o'clock
Meat 7 o'clock
Carrots 11 o'clock
Said his wife
They were fortunate. They had friends.
Friends that gave his wife a bit of work
As and when
Just enough to keep them ticking over
He was never going to work again
He knew that for sure
He knew he shouldn't have
He was only curious
What man wouldn't have been?
Why him though?
The other wives, they had been sensible
They had sent their men away for the day
But he had that job at the manor
And if you didn't do what the earl wanted
As and when he wanted
You would struggle to find work in the county again
Anyway she had always looked pretty before
Dressed in that fine silk and expensive jewellery
Just a quick glance he had thought
Not even a thought of a leer
Tom you're getting peas down your shirt
I understand Tom
I know you to be curious
But oh Tom, if only you hadn't peeped.

Coventry Childhood

Chris Hoskins

When I was a child
my father spoke about Coventry with fondness.
He'd revel at the 'craftsmanship' of a Raleigh bicycle
but I didn't understand.
Our family car, built here, gave my father excuses to tinker on
Sunday mornings.
For me, it was a squeeze for eight at a push.

My mother spoke about Coventry in sinister tones
A tainted vision in a frosted sky
The droning, diving for cover, charred remains.
But I never knew this place.
I didn't understand.

Now, I walk about this City
In cobbled stones I see their faces
hear sounds of hope
In museums I track my childhood
In tapestries I see
my jigsaw life held together
with the love that made them.

Only now do I understand.

The Ghost Walk

Maxine Burns

We met at Ma Browns, in Spon Street.

No one remembers her, but apparently she haunts her former pub. I was hoping she wasn't here. She was a right old witch.

Our ghost walker gave his name – it was Simon – and then asked ours. Everyone modestly supplied them and he head-counted, laughing affably, and said, "We don't want to lose anyone, do we?"

They tittered nervously, glancing shyly at each other. "Will we get on with it?" he asked, taking the words right out of my mouth.

We processed to St. Johns Church, where he recounted a little of its history – the civil war soldiers therein imprisoned. He mentioned the myth of 'sent to Coventry', which originated from this time and place. He prepared us for the ghost that he had hopes of seeing. A woman with a large bust looked around expectantly, then back, disappointed.

A beautiful woman appeared. She floated through the church door, wearing a black velvet cloak. On her head was a shining, golden crown.

Queen Isabella, I thought. Another old witch.

I began to raise my hand to gain attention, but although they were all looking, no one could see her. The Queen smiled at me, winked, and disappeared. By the time I had pulled myself together, the group had moved on, walking purposely towards Corporation Street. I had to put a spurt on, to catch up.

Simon counted heads again and began to tell us about the newly excavated site, behind the city's theatre. He waffled on, completely oblivious to a figure standing watching us. It was a monk. He was wearing a thick, black habit and I could see his yellow eyes, gleaming through the folds of his hood.

Next to me, a youngish man, in a yellow waistcoat, was sweating and shivery. My interest was piqued. Could he see the monk? No! He turned to a slender young woman and began chatting to her. Wasn't it exciting? – a real live ghost walk.

I went to touch his arm, to show him, but the monk waved and disappeared. The group was already on its way. I quickly followed.

By the time we reached Pepper Lane, my spirits had risen. Surely they would see something here. Perhaps sense a little of the dreadful ambience that infected this space? We trouped along the ancient cobbles, arriving at the river. I was chilled to the bone. The street was teeming with spirits. Wails filled the air. Long-dead babies clawed at the banks of the river, unable to grip the soft, loamy earth. Men and women hung from trees, clawing at ropes knotted around black, swollen necks, their legs thrashing, struggling for purchase.

Men were stabbing at empty air, their faces contorted with hatred and fear and despair.

I stood breathless and terrified as one of them noticed me and came lumbering towards me. I hurried to the middle of the group, like a fish in a shoal as a shark attacks.

They marched on, unaware.

We processed along Hales Street, and Simon nodded toward the old grammar school. "No sightings reported there," he said, failing to notice the thin, white-faced boys, peering through the windows, cheeky tongues pushed out, noses distorted, pressed against ghostly glass.

"But..." I shouted, feeling pretty desperate, "wait!" It was too late. We had arrived at the motor museum. We stood on the site of the old Hippodrome.

"The ghost of an actor who died on stage is seen from time to time," said Simon.

Elliot, the air raid warden, was watching the ghost walkers with interest. He bowed towards me, then melted into the dark recesses of Lady Herbert's Gardens. Was he meeting her? Mercifully, the gardens were of little interest to our ghost hunters and we made our way up the steps to Priory Row.

We gazed through toughened glass, to the excavation which had revealed an early monastery. A young monk spotted us and waved excitedly. The other, older monks carried on with their meal, chewing impassively, their faces registering no surprise. Suddenly, one of them spotted me. He rose, spat his food onto the earthen floor and started toward me. I backed away, unable to take my eyes from his blank, unforgiving face.

I nearly tripped over Simon and I quickly tagged on.

He was talking excitedly about Tony Robinson and the Time Team, as we made our way towards the cathedral, walking on old, uneven cobbles. I had to stand aside as a small horse, pulling a heavy cart, drove past us. A little girl, dressed in rags, stared as she went by. The noise was terrible. Unseen spectres shouted out prices for wares.

Drunken men – and women – were singing very rude songs. I heard flesh slapping against flesh, behind the ancient town walls. One man, carrying a heavy flagon of ale, stopped as he passed by, and turned to look at me. He grinned, revealing blackened, rotten teeth and pale, bloody gums. He mimed a smacking kiss as a low, awful growl rose from his throat.

"Great, isn't it?" said Simon.

I jumped, startled. The cacophony of sound had stopped abruptly, and his voice boomed in my ears. "Yes," I answered, smiling weakly.

We arrived at the old cathedral, and although gated and locked, we could see inside, through the wide, iron bars.

"On a certain night in November," said Simon, "if you listen very carefully, you can hear the Luftwaffe flying overhead, in a ghostly re-enactment of the blitz."

Was he being ironic? I wondered, as I was almost deafened by buzzing planes, the ack-ack of heavy artillery fire and bombs exploding – frighteningly near us.

I covered my ears and watched, as the others strained to hear something, anything. I was losing heart.

There was no ghostly figure holding her head under her arm when we passed St Mary's Hall. But as we reached the site of some long-demolished houses, I could see former occupants inside, enclosed by shimmering, ghostly walls. An elderly man and his wife were sitting by the fire, drinking tea. Next door, a large, coarse-looking man was drinking from a bottle of whisky.

At the end of the phantom row, a woman crouched, cornered, as a man towered above her, his face twisted in rage. He threw heavy punches into her soft belly, again and again. She looked up, saw me, and her eyes looked into mine, pleading, tears streaming down her gaunt, white face.

I shrugged, helplessly. She closed her eyes in despair. Her cries followed me as I ran on, to catch up.

The group stood, huddled together, looking at a large, Georgian house. Simon was giving details of its history and, as he spoke, I could see it taking place.

A short, bald man, running, knife in hand, after a shrieking woman.

A man, covered in blood, obviously dead, lay prone, a vicious cut running along his throat, almost decapitating him.

The knife-man stopped and turned to look at me, his eyes large, the colour of unripe gooseberries. The scene froze like a tableau. I stepped back.

A hand touched my arm and I jumped.

"Scary story, isn't it?" said Simon, grinning. "Nothing to worry about, though," he continued. "I have this." He waggled his eyebrows and produced a small, black box. "It's my ghost detector." A green light flashed. "It turns red when ghostly activity is nearby," he said.

I just looked, speechless.

We hurried on. Everyone was feeling cold and hungry. We passed the Martyrs' Cross, a red, fiery glow, with mercifully invisible, shrieking souls. The pungent smell of burning flesh followed, as we rounded the corner. When we arrived at the manor house, built for Queen Isabella, I didn't look to see if she was in. I had had enough.

We came, at last, to my house and stopped. I ran to the door and turned to wave goodbye. Simon was beginning another story.

"This was the home of Angela Bexley," he said.

I lowered my head, feeling shy.

"She died young, at the height of her fame."

I looked up, puzzled, as he went on.

"The house has been maintained as a museum, dedicated to her work. Shall we go in, take a look? You never know, she may be sitting at her desk, writing, as we speak."

He laughed, opened my front door, and one by one, they all walked right through me, into my house.

Sky Blue Soul

Jana Vera Greasley

Godiva glides through your silent streets
Hear the sound of Sanctuary's feet
Many faces over many years
The flee, the flurry, the escape from fear
The fear of persecution from religious foe
For the Templar, the Huguenot
From the Congo and Kosovo
Peace and reconciliation is victory's prize
Miracle of invention in a shining child's eyes
The beat of a Ska band, the march of Roman feet
The poetic legacy of Larkin's treats
Strange men destroy your symmetry
As your cathedral blows to smithereens like a leaf
St Michael defeats Satan in Christian belief
You are an old soul Coventry
Yet your spirit comes shining through
As the roar of the Whittle engine
Soars off into the big sky blue.

About the Authors

Margaret Egrot
Living with Lady G

I moved to Coventry in 1989. Work and family commitments kept me fully occupied for a couple of decades, and all the writing I did was work-related.

I started writing fiction in 2008 and joined the Coventry Writers' Group two years ago. Since then I have completed a novel for older teenagers, and a number of short stories.

I couldn't think of anything or anyone more associated with Coventry than the Lady Godiva story, but have tried to give a different viewpoint for this anthology.

Margaret Mather
Gallows Day

I grew up in Scotland and moved to Coventry in 1971 after becoming friends with a girl I met while we were both working in Norway. I worked at British Leyland and then Glass Coventry. I have four grandchildren and I am always on hand when needed to babysit. I now run my own business in distribution and logistics.

I started to write about 30 years ago. However, my job as a Sales Manager for a logistics company kept me fully occupied and my writing fell by the wayside. I have only recently started to write again and my greatest achievement – apart from winning 3rd prize for my stuffed kangaroo in the *Coventry Evening Telegraph* Craft Competition 1984 – was winning 2nd prize for my story in the Coventry Writers Competition this year. I can't begin to tell you what a thrill that was.

Mary Ogilvie
Remembrance and *Upon A Time*

I have been a member of the Coventry Writers' Group for over 30 years. For me the joy of being part of this society has been the pleasure of being with such creative people.

I have always looked on writing as a pastime rather than a way of earning a living although for a number of years I worked as a Grassroots

Reporter on the *Coventry Telegraph*, reporting on local news in my area, and I have always enjoyed writing articles over the years.

However, my greatest love is writing poetry and my poem *Remembrance* in the anthology was inspired by the ruins of Coventry Cathedral and what it might present to the onlooker. I hope you enjoy it.

Rosalie Warren
Wonders of the Coventry Ring

Rosalie Warren has had two novels for adults and one for young teens published in the last few years. A former university lecturer in AI and cognitive science, she now mainly does things to books (reads, writes, edits, proofreads, collects, dusts and occasionally recycles them), but hasn't yet been reduced to eating one. She is currently beginning a series for 7-9 year-olds, about a boy and his robot, and is also working on a science fiction novel for adults.

Her website is at http://www.rosalie-warren.co.uk and she blogs at http://rosalie-warren.blogspot.com/. As an occasional escape from the world of books, Rosalie likes to stroll by the sea and swim in it. She was born in Yorkshire and spent many years in Scotland, but has now lived in Coventry for a decade – almost long enough to understand the ring road, but not quite.

Martin Brown
This Town, *Pilgrims* and *The Horse's Tale*

Martin Brown is a Coventry kid, a regular contributor to Poets' Corner in the *Coventry Telegraph*, and author of two poetry books – *A Thousand Scary Cabbages* and *Shake Rattle and Custard* – both available in local bookshops and on t' internet. He claims to have once played 'Spin the Bottle' with Lady Godiva, during which she lost all her clothes and afterwards rode off in a huff – and little else.

Ann Evans
Inspired

I was born and bred in Coventry, my schools were All Souls Primary and Cardinal Wiseman Girls' Grammar, and I've worked at companies that seem just to be part of the city's history now – Wickman Machine Tools and British Leyland.

I began writing as a hobby when my three children were little. Now with grandchildren of my own, writing has turned into a full time career and a way of life. I have ten children's books published and two adult books to date. My latest children's book is *A Children's History of Coventry*, which I feel very privileged to have been commissioned to write.

My story, *Inspired*, is a spin off from my latest book, *Celeste* – a time-slip thriller for children. Watch out for more on *Celeste* on my website: www.annevansbooks.co.uk

Chris Jarvis
Coventry Unquiet

I am passionate about writing all kinds of things. My writing is regularly divided between stories, scripts, articles and the copywriting I try to sell to rich benefactors. Recently I have begun to see writing projects the way a sculptor must look at a block of stone. Surely, the final piece is in there somewhere, if only I can chip away all the bits that are hiding it...

Outside of writing, I have been a member of Coventry's *Wheatsheaf Players* for some years. I have written for and performed with the theatre many times. It's tucked away in Wyken and despite its being there for 30 years, many locals have not yet discovered this hidden gem.

Coventry Unquiet is the first of a series of Coventry-based ghost tales currently under development as an original radio serial to be recorded at the *Wheatsheaf Players'* theatre.

Ian Collier
Ghost Town and *A Message to You*

I have been writing on and off for many years and have attended several creative writing courses as my peripatetic careers permitted. I have co-authored several scientific works and a couple of reviews, but so far have had none of my fiction published.

I moved to the Coventry area around eight years ago and have worked in several schools in the city since then.

A Message To You was inspired by the 'Coventry Cat Woman'. *Ghost Town* came to me when I temped at Tower Court between jobs – after many years of being the black sheep of a family of Lancashire textile workers. It is the only time I ever worked at t' mill.

Calvin Hedley

A Question of Tears

I was born and brought up in Earlsdon, Coventry. Falling in the middle of a large family, I have six brothers and four sisters. Always having had poor eyesight, I was registered blind in 1983 and lost all vision in 1997. A graduate of Warwick University, I studied History and Politics. When aged thirty-eight, I relocated to County Durham in 2000, where I worked for the local authority, running a resource centre for visually impaired people. Having returned to the West Midlands in June 2011, my fiancée and I are due to be married in September. A member of Coventry Writers before my North East sojourn, I've recently rejoined the group. Interested in creative writing for some years, I am currently working on two novels. I also enjoy the discipline of short story writing. I have had a few small successes in creative writing competitions.

Sarah Boxwell

A Coventry Tale

At just ten years old, Sarah has been writing poems and short stories for as long as she can remember. It runs in the family: she is the daughter of local author Michael Boxwell, who has had more than a dozen books published in the last ten years, and a great niece to the American poet, Alan Hope.

Whilst still young, Sarah has been creating her own style and continually writes stories and poems, some of which are published on the Internet. She hopes to be an author when she grows up.

Gareth Layzell

Past Participants

Although I've never actually lived in Coventry I've always felt close ties to the city, beginning with being awed by the cathedral on a school trip from London in the mid-80s, and then continuing with regular trips to the city once I moved to the Midlands.

I've been writing all my life, but I've been taking it more seriously for the past fifteen years, clocking up two draft novels (one of which *Past Participants* links into), a mass of short stories, and more unfinished projects than I'd care to admit to. I tend to write Science Fiction, but have also been known to dabble in Urban Fantasy and Horror from time to time. My current project is a Western/Fantasy/Horror novel, which hopefully is not as eclectic as it sounds!

When I'm not writing or doing my day job (stuff with spreadsheets and databases, more interesting than it sounds but not worth getting into here), I'm usually messing around with video games, reading books or comics, or pretending that I can play the ukulele.

Derek Medcraft
The Stuff of Daydreams and *Tom*

I became interested in writing after attending a creative writing course at Henley College a few years ago, though this interest remained dormant until I joined the Coventry Writers' Group earlier in the year.

The Stuff of Daydreams and *Tom* are the first pieces I have ever had published. I'm sure I have several of my English teachers profoundly confused as to where they went right.

Chris Hoskins
Coventry Childhood

I am a poet, songwriter, singer and arranger and spend my time teaching, writing, performing or directing the choir One Voice, which is based in Coventry.

My poetry has been published in many literary magazines and anthologies, was commended in *Aesthetica* International poetry competition 2010, short-listed for the Leeds Peace Prize in 2006 and won the (Birmingham) Amnesty International prize for 2005.

I have also been commissioned to write for 'Poetry-on-Loan' postcards for the past three years. The postcards are available from all libraries in the West Midlands.

I have written and produced a successful series of monologues, *Relatively Speaking*, recorded on CD, which is available on loan in several libraries in the region and for sale.

My songs are performed by choirs and by 'Free Harmony', the *a cappella* trio I sing with. Our debut CD, *Off the beaten track* contains many original compositions and is on sale from www.chrishoskins.co.uk/products.html

The poem 'Coventry Childhood' grew as an idea, after moving to Coventry eleven years ago when I began to understand the link between the tapestry of my own life and the city.

Maxine Burns

The Ghost Walk

I have been a member of the Coventry Writers' Group for 30 years. During that time I have been chairman twice. The group has always been very supportive to the many writers we have seen over the years.

I personally enjoy writing short stories and articles, and have recently started writing a novel.

I am also co-writing a TV drama with another member of the group. I got the idea for my story in the anthology by a ghost walk around Coventry. Our city is so atmospheric it was difficult not to be inspired as we walked the cobbled streets of our old city.

I hope you enjoy the story.

Jana Vera Greasley

Sky Blue Soul

I'm a Cumbrian from Barrow in Furness and have lived in Coventry for the past twelve years. My interests are varied, ranging from the paranormal to cookery – and, of course, literature and poetry. My favourite authors are Edna O'Brien, John Updike and Truman Capote, and my favourite poets are Browning, John Betjeman and Larkin. I've been in the Coventry Writers' Group since the spring of 2011 and love meeting the talented writers, many of whom have been writing for years.

Hilary Morris

Cover Illustration

I am a self-taught artist and have lived in the Midlands all my life.

My first pen and ink sketches were sold at the local pub, after which I started to paint watercolours of the area and exhibited mainly at craft fairs.

Since retirement, I have had more time to improve my technique, resulting in great success combining soft watercolour washes with the crisp lines of pen and ink.

I recently held two exhibitions at Nuneaton Museum and Art Gallery, showcasing my paintings of the British coast. As well as seascapes, drawing old buildings is a passion of mine, so I was excited to be asked to submit artwork for the book, and thrilled when my design was chosen.

About the Coventry Writers' Group

Coventry Writers' Group is an informal and dynamic group of authors, journalists, poets and other writers based in the Coventry area. Some of us write professionally; many more are enthusiasts who write purely for pleasure.

Formed in the 1950s, the group exists to encourage and help writers. We meet once a month to discuss various aspects of writing, editing and publishing, and authors often read their work aloud for discussion.

As individuals, we write in a wide variety of styles and genres. Between us, we write poetry, plays, novels, short stories, magazine articles and factual works. What links us together is a passion for writing and a love of the written word.

If you enjoy writing and live locally, why not join in? It does not matter whether you are an accomplished writer or just starting out – new members are always welcome. Membership is free. Members get access to our web forums and we meet on the first Tuesday evening of each month in central Coventry (check our website for more details of our current venue).

www.CoventryWritersGroup.org.uk
info@CoventryWritersGroup.org.uk

Other Works by Local Authors

Shake, Rattle and Custard

50 poems to be read, recited or worn as a hat
Martin Brown

Martin Brown's latest book has won acclaim from critics and readers alike. Delightfully whimsical, it is full of short, entertaining poems that will lift your mood, make you think, or make you laugh out loud.

Charity's Child
Rosalie Warren

Published by Circaidy Gregory Press. Age range: 14-adult.
New eBook edition coming soon

A Virgin Birth?

It's 1984 and Charity Baker, aged 16, is pregnant. Who is the father of her child? Could it be Alan, assistant pastor of the Crabapple Christian fellowship? Or could the father, as Charity is claiming, actually be God? Charity's friend Joanne has her own reasons for needing an answer. But the truth, when it emerges, is dark enough to shake the strongest faith.

Time Crystal
Wyken Seagrave

There's a disaster at CERN in Switzerland and two men are absorbed by a black hole. Moments later time stops everywhere in the Universe except near fragments of mysterious blue crystal. Each one is surrounded by a bubble of time. Hold a crystal and you're alive. Without it, you're frozen in time.

The Beast

Ann Evans

Published by Usborne Publishing

Amanda is looking forward to her family camping holiday in
a remote Scottish valley. But as soon as she arrives with her
family she senses that something is wrong. Then Amanda
notices mysterious shadows flitting across the mountainside
and strange scratches on her brother.

   When an eccentric local man warns her that she should leave,
Amanda starts to believe that something is stalking her family. Soon she
realizes her worst nightmare has become a reality. She must fight to
protect those she loves...

The Traveller Stalls

An appreciation of Nuneaton Street Market

Barry Evans

Published by Code Green Publishing

The Traveller Stalls follows a mythical traveller who arrives in Nuneaton
and is captivated by the life and joy of the market town. The stories of the
traveller and the market intertwine for a day. Written as a narrative poem
and images of the market, this is a journey into the meaning of community.

Coping with Chloe

Rosalie Warren

Published by Phoenix Yard Books. Age range: 11+

Anna and Chloe are twins. They share everything – from
secrets to clothes; from fending off the school bully to
dealing with their parents' separation. Even Chloe's
terrible accident hasn't split them apart. After all, twins
have a special bond....

   But Anna is beginning to realise that being inseparable isn't always
easy. Especially when no one else seems to understand that Chloe isn't
really gone; no one apart from the dashing Joe that is, who, inconveniently,
seems to like both sisters.

A Children's History of Coventry

Discover history on your doorstep

Ann Evans

Published by Hometown World

Have you ever wondered what it would have been like living in Coventry when Lady Godiva was there? What about being a silk-weaver for the rich factory owners in Georgian times? This book will uncover the important and exciting things that happened in your town. With a helpful timeline, fun imaginary accounts, cool old photos of places you'll recognize in Coventry and amazing top facts and information, you will discover things in Children's History of Coventry you never knew about your town.

Harold Goes Underground

Christopher Bourne

Published by Rough Little Books

Follow the adventures of Harold – a glowing genetically engineered mouse who escapes from his keeper's cruel laboratory into London's Underground system!
Harold Underground is aimed at children aged 9 or over.

Relatively Speaking

A series of monologues

Chris Hoskins

Excerpts of reviews: "Beautifully simple, elegantly written and above all sincere....This audiobook of monologues reflect on personal and family relationships familiar to us all.....With a strong undercurrent of humour, the writing is reminiscent of Alan Bennett, whilst the performances are understated like overhearing a conversation." As reviewed by Hamish Glen, the Creative Director of Belgrade Theatre, and Victoria Wood.

90

Solar Electricity Handbook

The Electric Car Guide

Michael Boxwell

Published by Greenstream Publishing

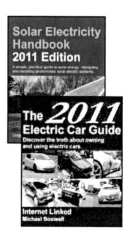

The world's best-selling book on solar energy and the world's best-selling book on electric cars have both been written by local author Michael Boxwell. Designer of numerous solar power systems and an electric car owner for more than five years, Michael's books explain both the technology and their uses in a clear and understandable way.

Free Harmony
Off the beaten track
Chris Hoskins

Free Harmony is an *a cappella* trio with a repertoire of original and world music, giving freedom to exquisite harmonies. The debut CD 'off the beaten track' includes several of Chris's original songs.

A Thousand Scary Cabbages and Other Curiosities

Martin Brown and Colin Baxter

A hugely entertaining book, suitable for both adults and children. The poetry is light-hearted, funny and suitable for children from the age of 5 to 100, whilst the superb artwork and illustrations make this the ideal gift book that will brighten up anybody's day.

Low Tide, Lunan Bay

Rosalie Warren

Published 2009 by Robert Hale Ltd. Age Range: Adult

Abbie has come through a difficult divorce and is trying to build a new life in Dundee with her 11-year-old twin girls. Her friend Kate persuades her to try internet dating and she meets Bill. Their first date, which includes a walk across beautiful Lunan Bay, goes well and Abbie is optimistic.

But when the twins start to have nightmares and behave badly at school, Abbie can't help wondering if her new relationship with Bill is somehow responsible.

When the truth emerges, it is far from anything Abbie expected and strains the family to breaking point.

Little Tyke Murder Mysteries: Fishing For Clues, Stealing The Show, Pushing His Luck, Pointing the Finger

Ann Evans

Originally published by Scholastic Children's Books, now available as Kindle eBooks on Amazon.

Who doesn't love a good murder mystery story? This Little Tyke Murder Mystery series by children's author, Ann Evans, provides four great whodunnits for younger readers to enjoy.

Each crime story is packed with mystery and adventure.

These eBooks for children allow the young readers to look for clues among the red herrings and work out who committed the crime. This series of kids eBooks comes with a web link to some secret pages containing author tips on deciding who the culprit is.

Make an eBook

The complete handbook for creating, marketing and selling eBooks successfully.

Michael Boxwell

Published by Greenstream Publishing

Make an eBook explains how to publish a book as an eBook from scratch, taking your document, preparing it convert to Kindle and other formats, getting it on sale and ensuring you get a book you can be proud of.

The handbook then goes on to show how to promote and sell your eBook around the world.

I Love to Sing

Chris Hoskins

Rounds and short pieces for all singers regardless of their singing experience. The rounds start simply, becoming more difficult as they progress through the CD and act as an introduction to harmony singing. The CD helps development of active listening skills; pitching; rhythm development; keeping time and may be incorporated into a vocal warm-up routine.

Lightning Source UK Ltd.
Milton Keynes UK
UKOW050618311011

181214UK00001B/3/P